LEISURE DYING

Other books by the author

THE BABY MERCHANTS
DIAL 577 R-A-P-E
DON'T WEAR YOUR WEDDING RING
THE PHONE CALLS
DIVE INTO DARKNESS
THE FACE OF THE CRIME
THE TACHI TREE
THE SLEEPING BEAUTY MURDERS
THE BABES IN THE WOODS
DEATH OF A PLAYER
MURDER UNDER THE SUN
DEATH SCHUSS
DEATH BLANKS THE SCREEN
DEATH ON THE GRASS

LEISURE
DYING
by Lillian O'Donnell

G. P. Putnam's Sons
New York

COPYRIGHT © 1976 BY LILLIAN O'DONNELL

SBN: 399-11741-5

Library of Congress Cataloging in Publication Data

O'Donnell, Lillian.
  Leisure dying.

  (Red mask mystery)
  I. Title.
PZ4.0254Le   [PS3565.D59]   813'.5'4   75-43795

PRINTED IN THE UNITED STATES OF AMERICA

Grow old along with me!
The best is yet to be,
The last of life, for which the first was made.

—ROBERT BROWNING

1

THE JOGGER entered Central Park at West Sixty-seventh Street. He was distinctive—big, over six feet tall, and close to two hundred pounds in weight—and he wore a bright red warm-up suit with a white stripe down each arm and each leg, yet nobody paid particular attention to him. The mothers with children felt safe behind the iron palings of the playground enclosure; the old people, sprawled on the benches like bundles of laundry waiting to be picked up, averted their eyes— fearing the young, not daring even to look at them; the dog walkers were concerned with keeping watch for the police while their animals cavorted illegally off leash. No one gave the jogger a second glance.

He crossed the road and headed east, moving at a slow, even, plodding pace, his sneakers silent on the cement path.

The night's heavy rain had continued into morning, stopping around ten. Now at last the sun was out, a bleak November sun with little warmth in it and not enough strength to dry the puddles choked with newly fallen leaves. The vast, open expanse of the Sheep Meadow was largely mud; one badly eroded area had been turned into a lake on which half a dozen ducks floated as placidly as though it were their natural habitat. Here there were no people at all. It was much too early for the children's sporting clubs—organizations which under the guise of teaching and supervising team sports such as field hockey, football, and baseball actually served as baby-sitters for affluent parents—they would come after school, if they showed up at all on such a day. The hot dog and bagel vendors wouldn't appear unless there were customers.

1

The jogger slowed. His feet dragged. His breath came in uneven grunts, condensing into little puffs in front of him. His affable but vapid face was covered with sweat. He hated jogging and was considering taking a break when he caught sight of his friends up ahead on the other side of the Mall. It cost him a considerable effort, but he quickened his pace. They wouldn't like to be kept waiting.

They saw him, too, but they had no intention of going out to meet him. Lounging against the edge of the bandstand, smoking their cigarettes, they pretended not to notice him as long as the police car moved cautiously along the pedestrian path. If the day continued to improve, there would be more patrol cars, helmeted police on scooters, and at dusk, regardless of weather, the area would be at patrol saturation. For now the one car made its cursory tour of the Mall and exited back to the roadway just above the Bethesda Fountain. When it was gone, the two in the royal-blue suits squashed out their cigarettes and sauntered lazily toward the jogger in red.

They were brothers, Duncan and Brett, both small, dark, nervously thin, with young, fresh faces and eyes, already old, that darted restlessly, searching without knowing what they were looking for. There had been no need to wait for the police car to leave; it didn't matter whether or not they were seen together, but Duncan, the smaller of the two, never missed a chance to make the big guy squirm.

"You're late," he challenged.

"Sorry, Dunc. I wasn't sure . . . I mean, the weather. . . ."

"This is the best kind of weather. You ought to know that by now."

"I'm sorry."

"Okay, okay. So what are we waiting for? Let's move out. There's no action here."

At that moment a lone man, well dressed, carrying a briefcase, emerged from the rest-room building, heading toward them. He appeared to be in his late thirties, and his pace was brisk and energetic. Duncan shrugged, and the other two immediately lost interest.

"How about the Ramble?" It was an order, not a question, and Duncan moved off.

"Why not?" Brett followed.

2

The jogger in red mutely accepted their decision and hurried to catch up.

The three crossed the road then took the long, broad flight of steps down to the esplanade. Turning left on the lake path toward the Bow Bridge, they began jogging, but not in single file—abreast, so that they filled the width of the path and no one could get by them.

The park was Horace Pruitt's refuge and his solace. The Ramble, an intricate maze of paths that dipped and turned between the lake and the great meadow, that climbed small hillocks and plunged into miniature valleys, wound around mock ruins, and skirted artfully placed boulders, was his favorite area. Here Pruitt could imagine that he was out of the city, really in the woods. Of course, in spring and summer, when the trees were in full leaf, it was easier to sustain the illusion, for then the buildings surrounding the park were screened out. Forty years in the city and Horace Pruitt still yearned for the woods of Vermont.

He was already middle-aged when he came to New York with his wife, Amy, and the two boys. He had intended to stay only a few years, just long enough to make the money to buy back the farm he'd lost during the Depression, or one like it. He'd been lucky, got a job as an apprentice printer, learned the trade, went into business for himself, did well, yet was never able to set enough aside. He made more money than he ever had before in his life, but everything cost more, and there were emergencies always. Somehow the years passed; suddenly he was old and alone. The boys had died in Korea; Amy was gone. He sold the business, but the proceeds were used up by her long illness and the funeral costs. He had Social Security though, and the apartment was rent-controlled. He wasn't as badly off as some.

To fill in the long, empty days Pruitt had started coming to the park. He came early, at first light, and one day he fell in with a bird-watching group. He started making sketches, then later, when he was home in his empty apartment, and again to fill time, he translated the rough sketches into wood carvings. A forgotten skill of his youth, his early efforts were crude, but as his stiff fingers limbered, the work improved, engrossed

3

him, and the collection of birds and small woodland creatures, some observed in the park and some remembered from the Vermont woods, proliferated. They filled his two and a half rooms, perching on shelves and tables. Rather than relegate them to boxes and closets, he gave them to his neighbors in the building till inevitably someone suggested that he sell them. With considerable trepidation, Horace Pruitt packed a few of his best examples and offered them to an antique and gift shop, one of many that had recently sprung up on Columbus Avenue. They were accepted and quickly sold. Now he had four outlets for the carvings and derived a variable but respectable income from the work. He was eighty-two. Living frugally and with no outside demands on him, Horace Pruitt had every expectation of going back to Vermont at last.

This morning, as soon as the rain let up, Pruitt had come out to the Ramble as usual, and as usual he carried his sketch pad and his lunch. The sketching finished, lunch over, the rise of the hill sheltering him from the gusty wind, he leaned against a sun-warmed rock and looked out over the newly restored Bow Bridge, which spanned the narrow neck between boat basin and lake. Already the shadows were falling on the water as the sun sank behind the Gulf + Western building, but it would be another half hour before they reached his aerie. He would have liked to stay that extra half hour, but he had work waiting at home and marketing and housecleaning to do before he could get to the work. Being a disciplined man with a goal, Pruitt got up, stretched lazily, and started down the hill toward the lake. As he did so, he noticed three boys in jogging outfits—one in red and two in blue—crossing the Bow Bridge and heading toward him. He smiled because he liked to see the young people out exercising: It was an indication that some of them were aware of natural pleasures, could find enjoyment away from city streets. They seemed uncertain which way to go. Probably they wanted to ask him for directions. He was still smiling when they met at the foot of the bridge.

"Hey, mister, give me a dollar."

Pruitt was taken aback. "What for?"

The speaker wore blue and was the smallest of the trio. He was thin and awkward as a puppy with arms and legs that had

4

grown faster than the rest of him and to which he had not yet accommodated. There the similarity ended. He smiled at Pruitt, but it was not a nice smile. "Because I want it."

Horace Pruitt was not easily frightened, and he wasn't frightened now. They were only kids, showing off to one another, probably on a dare. It was a game. No doubt they stopped lots of people and even made a few dollars; but it was a nasty game, and he had no intention of encouraging them in it. "That's no reason," he retorted, and shifted to step past. Instantly the other two took up positions on either side of the boy who had made the demand, blocking Pruitt's way.

"Give me a dollar." The smile had turned into a sneer; the eyes were calculating.

"Why should I?" Pruitt stood his ground. It was the only thing to do. With these kids you had to be firm, show them you weren't afraid.

"Why make a big deal out of it, mister? It's only a dollar."

"You're a real cheapskate, you know that?" the second one in blue joined in. "Why don't you give it to him? He's asking you nice and polite."

Only the big one, the one in red, said nothing.

A cold chill passed through Horace Pruitt; he shivered. He'd heard of gangs of youths beating up old, defenseless bums and winos, picking their victims by some mindless lottery—such as going up to a prospect and asking for a match. If the person had it and offered it, they passed on. Otherwise. . . . Never having expected that he would himself be approached, Pruitt had not considered what he might do in such an eventuality. He took a quick look around. There was nobody in sight, nobody. He was far from feeble, he could fight, but they were three and they were young. Could he turn and run? How far would his old legs carry him?

As though reading his thoughts, two of the three repositioned themselves slightly behind so that with the small one still in front, Pruitt found himself at the center of a triangle and even that slight chance of escape was cut off.

"I'm sorry, I don't have a dollar." He was ashamed to be so meek, but he was now, finally, afraid.

"Don't lie, old man."

"I'm not lying, I swear. I don't have it. I don't have any

money on me at all. Not even a wallet. I never carry money when I come to the park. That's the God's truth."

The first blow caught him at the side of the head just below his right ear. His brain felt as though it had been jarred loose from his skull; his teeth ached; his vision blurred. Instinctively his arms went up to protect his head, and then the blows rained on his body. He went down to his knees, hunching in on himself. They beat him on the back. They were all around him and over him. Still in pain from that first brutal blow, disoriented and off-balance because of the humming in his ears, not daring to raise his head, he nevertheless saw a sneakered foot drawn back, aiming at his groin. He threw himself on it; grabbing the ankle, clutching it, and using all his weight, he pulled that particular attacker down and somehow managed to sprawl on top of him. He stayed there. Pruitt was a heavy man, and there wasn't much to the boy. Pruitt's weight was sufficient to keep him pinned.

"Get him off me. Get him off!" Duncan screeched.

The beating stopped. As hands pulled at Pruitt's coat collar, the boy underneath him squirmed and heaved to get free. Hardly knowing what he was about, reacting instinctively, Horace Pruitt's hands, his strong wood-carver's hands, found the youth's throat.

"He's choking me. Help . . . help. . . ." The plea turned into a series of strangled gasps.

Hands tore at his arms, but Pruitt's grip tightened. "Go away," he grunted. "The two of you go away from me and I'll let him go. Not before." His strength was failing. He didn't know how much longer he could last, long enough, he hoped, for someone to come and help or at least to give the alarm.

"Don't just stand there, for Chrissake!" the second boy exhorted the one in red. "Give me a hand. He's killing Dunc. Can't you see he's choking Dunc to death?"

With a different kind of terror, Horace Pruitt now realized that the boy underneath him had stopped struggling, that he was lying limp and still. Yet he couldn't let go. His hands were rigidly locked around the boy's throat. He had no power to remove them. He watched in horror as the boy's face turned purple, as he gasped for air.

6

"Come on, Rick, come on, man, help me," the boy cried as he continued his futile efforts.

In the next moment Pruitt felt the boy pulled off his back and strong arms lock around his chest. They tightened. Then he was hoisted up and off the prone youth, raised a couple of feet into the air, and held there. But still he couldn't let go. Still his hands retained their grip; his fingers would not uncurl. Then he was shaken, methodically, relentlessly, and with such power that he thought if he did not close his eyes, they would fall out of his head. The tremors passed into his fingers at last, and somehow the death grip was loosed. At the same moment that Horace Pruitt let go, a scream sounded from somewhere up in the woods behind them.

The scream paralyzed them all. The boy on the ground did not pick himself up; the one holding Pruitt stopped shaking him. Finally the screaming stopped.

Brett kneeled beside his brother. "Dunc? Dunc? You okay?"

"The fucking old man nearly killed me," Duncan rasped. "Well, what are you waiting for?" he demanded. "Hit him. Hit him."

Rick still held Pruitt like a sack he didn't quite know where to put down.

There was a second scream, closer this time. A dog barked hysterically. A police siren bleeped from somewhere across the lake.

"Kill him, Rick. Kill him!" Duncan snarled as he got up.

The police car cut off the road to the path, was circling the lake, making good speed.

"It's too late." His brother tugged at Duncan's arm. "It's too late. We gotta split."

The dog was on them, darting in an out between their legs, yapping, barking.

The police car had got as far as the Bow Bridge, but because of the metal posts embedded at either end, the vehicle couldn't cross.

"Kill him!" Duncan screamed.

Horace Pruitt felt himself jerked erect. He was turned around and held by the front of his shirt at arm's length. He saw the blow coming, the fist clenched, the arm pulled back.

7

He flinched and turned his head aside. He heard an animal snarl, then before the blow was struck, he heard a yelp of pain. His own? Unrecognizable. The last things he saw were the lake and trees of his beloved retreat with the spires of the city curving up and around as though the whole were encased in an old-fashioned paperweight. Then someone turned the paperweight upside down.

2

SERGEANT NORAH MULCAHANEY caught the squeal. As soon as she heard that the victim was still alive, without bothering to wait for the elevator, she ran down the stairs and out of the precinct house. Eighty-second Street was choked with cars parked on both sides—a bone of contention between Traffic Division and the detectives to whom most of the cars belonged—but Norah had no trouble spotting hers. It was the first car she'd ever owned, and she felt an inordinate pride in it. Norah had always considered that men were childishly infatuated with their automobiles, yet from the moment she'd entered the showroom, she'd begun to behave just as irrationally. There was no use denying that when she got behind the wheel of the dark moss-green Pinto, Norah Mulcahaney Capretto experienced a sense of freedom and identity that, despite the fact that she was holding down a good job and making good money, she hadn't felt since she and Joe had married.

They had a good marriage, Norah and Lieutenant Joseph Antony Capretto; they were happy. Norah would have been the first to deny, and hotly, that she existed in her husband's shadow. She hadn't resigned her own personality or been

8

absorbed into his—either at home or at work. On the contrary, Norah felt that she had grown and developed since her marriage. She had joined the force when she was twenty-eight, still unsure of herself, still searching for direction. She was the one who fell in love first; at least, she was the one first aware of being in love.

In those days Joseph Antony Capretto had been somewhat of a swinger. Handsome, tall, dark, with a noble Roman profile and accompanying Latin charm, he had dated a string of glamorous models and stewardesses. Norah knew that she was older than most of his girls and certainly not in their league for looks. Oh, she was attractive enough, but in a quiet, unobtrusive way. Heads didn't turn when Norah entered a restaurant. She was tall, slim enough, but too sturdy to be whistled at, often anyway. She had the fine Irish coloring: pale skin, dark, nearly black hair, and blue-gray eyes with long, naturally thick lashes. Unfortunately these good points were marred by a square, much too prominent jaw which she was in the habit of thrusting out in moments of stress. Since she wasn't his type and didn't seem interested in becoming another of Sergeant Capretto's conquests, Norah Mulcahaney had tried to suppress her feeling, dismissing it as a crush, the natural admiration of a rookie policewoman for a handsome superior officer who had been nice to her.

But Capretto had been more than nice. He had given Norah Mulcahaney guidance and the chance to show what she could do. The fact that she had proved equal to the opportunity and had made detective wasn't the point. Making detective was still a hit-or-miss business; some officers waited for years for the chance to show their mettle, others never got the chance at all. Then and now, being a detective meant everything to Norah, and she felt she owed it all to Joe.

As for Joseph Antony, he couldn't have said when he started to think of the rookie policewoman romantically. Admittedly he overreacted when she was in danger, but he rationalized that as a natural concern for any woman under his command. That didn't explain, however, the twinges of jealousy he felt when Detective Mulcahaney showed a more than professional interest in the men she worked with. . . . Specifically there had been a certain assistant DA. Nor did

9

it explain his own spurt of ambition. For eleven years Joe had been a detective sergeant—a good, satisfying job, financially adequate. Suddenly he'd started to think about advancement, about the future. Certainly he expected to get married—sometime. Approaching forty, a bachelor with a doting mother to care for him, thoughts of marriage were becoming nebulous. It wasn't till Norah Mulcahaney entered his life that he began to wonder if he might be missing something. He even wondered whether his attitude might be somewhat immature! He began studying for the lieutenant's exam and courting Norah at the same time.

Joe's love fulfilled Norah, made her confident as a woman, less afraid to show tenderness, and at the same time imparted a degree of sophistication. Married to Norah, Joe Capretto didn't have to be flaunting his manhood constantly. They complemented each other; they grew individually and as a couple.

To avoid confusion, Norah still used her maiden name on the job; she was Sergeant Mulcahaney. That she would continue to work was agreed between them, and their work was a strong bond. At first they had worked the same shifts but out of separate commands, then Joe was transferred from Narco to the Fourth Homicide and became Norah's commanding officer. There was no strain. It wasn't the first time Norah had worked for Joe, not even the first time since their marriage. She followed her husband's orders as she would those of any superior—with the same respect but also with plenty of independent expression of her own ideas. If she'd stopped to think about it, if either of them had, each would have agreed that they worked well together, better than with anyone else, that the emotional tie seemed to add strength to the professional.

Because the call was so urgent, Norah skipped the usual walk-around assessment of her car and got right in. The motor responded with satisfying promptness and smooth power. Yet as she edged out into the street, her elation was marred by a twinge of guilt. Lately she'd begun to look on this freedom of spirit as a disloyalty to Joe. He put no strings on her, no limits to her growth. On the contrary, everything she was—the woman she had become, as well as her police rank—

was because of him. She had been advancing steadily from detective third grade to second to first, but it was Joe who had urged her to go out for sergeant.

They had no children, so after two years of marriage they'd decided to adopt a son. The questionable legality of the adoption had been used by the mob to blackmail Joe Capretto. Realizing that the uncertainty about their right to keep young Mark would hang over them for the rest of their lives, certainly make it impossible for either of them to function as police officers, Norah had made the only possible decision and given the boy up. By this time it wasn't her own career that mattered but Joe's, as well as the child's future security. It was the hardest thing she'd ever done in her life. The aftermath for her was a period of lethargy and sorrow that she couldn't seem to shake off. Even now she occasionally fell into troughs of despondency, but they were leveling off. Deeply stricken himself, Joe's concern was all for her. One day, he prayed, they would have a child of their own, meantime . . . he suggested to his wife that she take the sergeant's exam.

For Norah it was therapy. For Joe it meant long nights of watching television in the living room while his wife studied in the dining room, lonely Saturday nights, and dreary Sundays. He never complained. He had encouraged Norah. And his pleasure when she was appointed, one of the last before the mayor's budget cutback in civil-service promotions, was as great as hers. Even the car had been Joe's idea.

"You're a sergeant now and you should have wheels of your own."

They were still using the car of Joe's bachelor days as the family car. They rode to work in it together, crossing through the park via the Sixty-seventh Street transverse from their East Side apartment to the West Side precinct house; after that it was allocated according to need.

"I thought we'd decided to replace the Mustang."

"Are you kidding? I've just about got it broken in," Joe had replied with mock indignation.

So it was silly to feel guilty about the car. The car was not an indication of restlessness or subconscious dissatisfaction with her marriage or her way of life. It was a novelty, and a novelty that would wear off soon enough.

11

Entering the park at Seventy-second, Norah put aside all stray thoughts to concentrate on the job ahead. Mugging had become an ordinary crime, Norah knew, and nobody gets excited anymore about a mugging—except the victim. Very little effort is expended in investigating a mugging precisely because there are so many of them; they happen every day many times over, in every part of the city to all kinds of people, rich and poor, white and black. Nowadays a victim is considered lucky if all he suffers is a loss of money or valuables. Most often he gets a bad beating; a woman may be raped— seemingly at whim, whether or not resistance is offered, and apparently regardless of the amount of money involved. Violence for the sake of violence—it both revolted and saddened Norah Mulcahaney. Apparently this attack was one of the really vicious kind. All she knew was that the victim was male, that he had been severely and perhaps fatally assaulted. In the usual course, street muggings were the responsibility of the local precinct investigating unit, and in accordance with the recent pass-along system, Homicide would be called only if and when the victim died. That could mean a delay of hours or days. There was a saying that the chances of solving a murder cool off faster than the corpse. So the uniformed officer had shown good judgment in notifying Homicide as soon as he realized that the victim was near death. Because of his quick thinking, it might even be possible for Norah to get a statement.

She hurried, swinging off the road and onto the grass verge so she could go against traffic directly to the parking area. She got out and walked to the top of a small rise from which there was a good view of the lake and environs. But Norah was not interested in the topography, not when she saw that the ambulance was already there and that the attendants would be removing the victim shortly.

"Hold it!" she shouted. "Wait." She was gasping and had a sharp stitch in her side from running when she reached the small group around the prostrate man. "Sergeant Mulcahaney, Fourth Homicide," she said, identifying herself. "Just give me a couple of seconds, please."

A man moved to one side, and she knelt beside the victim.

He was old, an old, old man. His face was swollen and

12

discolored from the beating; the back of his head was covered with blood already darkened and caking. Norah felt sick, sick with pity and sick to her stomach. As many times as she saw the aftermath of violence she never got used to it, and she had resigned herself to the fact that she never would. How could anyone do this to a helpless old man? He was unconscious, appeared barely to be breathing. There wouldn't be any statement—not now, if ever. She got up and motioned to the orderlies to go ahead: She didn't want to cause even one more second's delay.

She watched as they lifted him carefully and laid him on the stretcher, but as soon as he was strapped in, she turned away. Her job now was to find out who had done it.

If this were a homicide, the area would have been crowded with cars and swarming with detectives and a full complement of technical personnel to examine the scene and record every nuance of the crime. Norah was very conscious of their absence and the responsibility this placed on her. She would have to try to cover their functions. She took a deep breath, held it, then slowly let it out again. The first thing was to study the layout.

The victim had been lying on the cement path about fifteen feet from the bridge and ten feet from a small gazebo, with the water on one side and a wooded hill rising steeply on the other. Inside the gazebo, half hidden in shadow, there appeared to be a woman. A witness? Norah would interview her later, after she got the story from the two radio-car officers.

Their names were on the new tags worn beneath their shields. "Rosoff? Carson? I'm Sergeant Mulcahaney."

They were both young, with a good healthy bloom in their cheeks. They looked well padded, particularly about the hips, but that was probably because of the heavy underwear most men who drew outdoor duty put on. They shook hands all around. "So what happened?" she asked.

Rosoff answered. "We were cruising along with the regular park traffic." He pointed to the road above and on the other side of the lake. "We heard a woman scream. We got off the road and started down when we spotted these three guys beating up on the old man."

Three! Norah thought. No wonder he looked like that.

13

"We turned the siren on, but it didn't mean a thing to them," Rosoff continued bitterly. "I mean, I can see where some woman screaming would hardly scare them off, but a police siren? That should have stopped them, shouldn't it?" he appealed to Norah. "It didn't. They kept right on hitting him, just kept right on knocking him around."

Norah looked to the other side of the arched bridge. The ambulance was long since gone, and only Rosoff and Carson's patrol car remained, with both front doors wide open.

"They split before we got out of the car, Sergeant. Maybe we should have stopped and fired from the other side. But the distance . . . the risk of hitting the victim. . . ."

He was not alibiing; he was genuinely questioning the course of action he and his partner had taken. Norah sympathized, but made no comment. Let it all hang out, she thought. It would help put Officer Rosoff at ease, allowing her to get a good picture of exactly what had occurred.

"We're not supposed to fire warning shots, you know." Rosoff continued his bitter review of the events. "A wild bullet could injure an innocent bystander, but there were no bystanders. I could have fired into the water. It might have scared them away before they finished him off." Rosoff took a deep breath. "What I'm telling you, Sergeant, is that when we got down to the water's edge, the old man was still on his feet. The kid in red was holding him by his shirtfront, but he was on his feet."

It was a catharsis for Rosoff, but his partner didn't like it. "We figured to drive right up and grab them; that's why we didn't take time to stop and fire." Carson realized he'd made matters worse. "We forgot about those lousy posts." He pointed ruefully to the posts that blocked access to vehicles. "All that money to restore the dumb bridge, then they put those posts in so that a car can't get through."

"Did you get a good look at the perpetrators?" Norah asked.

"We only saw them from the back," Rosoff explained. "They were wearing sweat suits—two blue and one bright red. They all had dark hair, kind of an in-between length. The two in blue were skinny, medium height. The one in red was big, over six feet, and heavy, say about two-ten. The old man was down, and this punk in red just hauled him up to his feet like

14

he was nothing. He held him up for that last punch, then dropped him on the cement. You saw the back of his skull—it just cracked open like an egg."

The blood and matter had already seeped into the pavement, and all that remained was a dark, enigmatic stain. The three officers stared at it as though it could tell them something.

"I stayed with the victim," Rosoff concluded. "Ev—Officer Carson—went in pursuit."

Norah turned inquiringly to Carson.

He shrugged. "They scrambled up the hill and fanned out in different directions." He was as disturbed as Rosoff but for different reasons. "That damn Ramble! There's just too much cover in there, too many twists and turns and hills and dales. They ought to clear out the whole area."

"I assume you put out an alarm," Norah said.

"Yes, ma'am, right away, but we haven't heard anything. If there hasn't been a report by now, well, they haven't been picked up. And if they haven't been picked up, they're out of the park." Carson scowled. "What gets me is the nerve of those punks wearing those bright outfits. It's like they're thumbing their noses at us."

"There must be plenty of those outfits around," Norah observed.

"Sure." Carson looked at Norah as though she weren't very bright. "The point is you can spot them a mile off."

"Maybe that's the idea. All they'd have to do is pull off the jacket and the pants and they could walk right by you without your giving them a second glance."

Carson and Rosoff stared at her.

"The only thing is, muggers, ordinary muggers, don't usually go to that much trouble." She frowned, then glanced toward the gazebo, where the woman she'd noted earlier still patiently waited. A couple more minutes shouldn't matter. "Let's get back to the victim. Was he conscious when you reached him?"

"No, Sergeant." Before, Rosoff had been venting his frustration; now he was supplying information to a superior. "From the way he hit the pavement I was surprised he was still breathing."

15

"How about ID?"

"He didn't have a wallet on him, but he did have a couple of letters." The officer consulted his notebook. "One was addressed to Horace Pruitt. That one was a bill and the other was addressed to 'resident' but the number and street were the same. Both were postmarked four days back. I figure Pruitt picked up his mail on the way out, stuffed it into his pocket, and forgot about it."

Norah nodded. "Let's have the address."

Having noted it, she now turned to examine the area over which Carson had indicated the muggers had fled. The ground was still soggy and should have taken prints. Norah bent down, searching. There were prints, all right, but badly messed up—probably by Officer Carson. She could hardly blame him for not thinking about prints while he was in hot pursuit. Anyhow, since the three had fled in different directions, there should be two unspoiled sets. She made a mental note to get a photographer over; it might also be worthwhile to have someone from the lab make casts. . . . Meanwhile, she moved up the hill, careful where she put her own feet. Suddenly she stopped and bent down to examine a clump of grass that was still a healthy green. There were dark spots on the tips of the blades. She touched one such spot with a finger. Tacky. Looking closer, she saw that the spots were pear-shaped rather than round, with the narrow end pointing up the hill. She found more patches of grass spotted in the same manner. "Did you fire?" she called down to Carson.

"No, ma'am. They were out of sight before I had the chance."

"Which one did you follow?"

"The big one, the guy in red. He was the one that did the damage."

She pointed to the spots. "He was bleeding."

Rosoff and Carson looked at each other. "The dog," they said with one accord.

"What dog?"

"Hers. The woman who screamed." Rosoff pointed to the woman in the gazebo. "The dog was right in the thick of it, yapping at their heels. I guess he took a bite out of Red."

Carson grinned. "Feisty little mutt."

16

Obviously they hadn't got the witness' statement. A lot had happened, and happened fast. Norah didn't want to appear to reprimand them, particularly as they were already smarting from having failed to apprehend even one of the muggers. "Why don't I just go over to her and talk with her quietly, woman to woman? Make it easier for her to loosen up."

Rosoff took the remark at face value. "She probably would feel easier with you, Sergeant."

Carson wondered why she bothered to explain. "Whatever you say, ma'am."

Norah flushed. She had meant to be considerate, but it had come out as though she were asking their permission. She was too aware of others' feelings, too anxious for their good opinion. It was about time she learned to do the job without apologizing. Without another word, she marched over to the gazebo.

It was one step down from the path and one step above the gently lapping water. Its low rustic roof kept out the sun and forced Norah to duck her head in order to see inside. The woman sitting on the wooden bench was bundled up in a shabby fur coat, species no longer identifiable, and wore a black woolen cap pulled down to her eyebrows. A few wisps of white fuzz escaped on either side. Her face was completely crisscrossed with lines deep as knife cuts. Her pallor was so ghostly it seemed impossible that the blood that nourished her could be red. She paid no attention to Norah; she was completely engrossed with her dog. It had the body of a small German shepherd, but the legs were short and the jowls heavy. Its rheumy eyes indicated it was not a young dog. The old lady obviously adored it. Leaning over, she stroked it, murmuring to it in a low, soothing voice.

"Hello, I'm Sergeant Mulcahaney." Norah held out her ID so the witness could take all the time she wanted to examine it, which she did, then tilted her head up sideways to get a good look at Norah with eyes that were small but bright and alert.

"You're a detective, dear? Isn't that nice?"

Norah was prepared to be patronized, resented, admired, but she had never before been praised like a bright child. "Well, yes, I like it."

"And I'm sure you're very good at it, dear."

17

"Thank you, I try to be. And you're Mrs. . . ?"

"Youngbeck, dear. Cordelia Youngbeck. This is Lady." She indicated the dog.

"Hello, Lady."

"She'll shake hands if you ask her."

Norah took time to do that, and the dog, panting heavily, managed to lift a limp paw. "Is she all right?"

"I hope so. She's had a lot of excitement; it's not good for her heart. She's not as young as she used to be."

Norah bit back a smile. "I'm sorry to have kept you waiting, Mrs. Youngbeck."

"That's all right. I don't have anything else to do." Though she wore so many clothes, the old lady shivered.

"It's very damp here," Norah observed. "Why don't we go over to the cafeteria and get some hot coffee?"

"Well . . . I didn't bring any change with me."

"It's on the department." Norah didn't think she would accept if she thought it was coming out of Norah's own pocket.

"Oh. In that case. . . ."

"Good. Actually, I haven't had lunch yet. Maybe you'd join me?"

There was longing in Mrs. Youngbeck's eyes, but her pride won out. "Thank you. I've eaten."

Norah doubted it. "Won't you just have something to keep me company? A snack? My mother-in-law says that the 'appetite comes with the eating.' That's a rough translation."

"It's very kind of you. All right."

"I'll just make a note of your name and address and pass it on to the officers for the report."

That done, Sergeant Mulcahaney, Cordelia Youngbeck, and Lady crossed the Bow Bridge and strolled along the path to the low brick building overlooking the end of the boat basin. It took awhile because slow as Mrs. Youngbeck was, the dog was even slower. When they reached the cafeteria, there was another problem: The dog was not permitted inside and Mrs. Youngbeck absolutely refused to tie Lady up and leave her.

"Somebody might steal her."

The difficulty was resolved by Norah's going in to get the food and bringing it out. They sat on a bench in the lee of the

18

building, warmed by the last rays of the autumn sun, and ate. Half of Mrs. Youngbeck's roast beef sandwich was surreptitiously slipped to Lady. Norah pretended not to see, suspecting that to be the real reason the old woman hadn't wanted to go in without her dog. Norah offered to get another sandwich, but Mrs. Youngbeck would not accept.

Norah leaned back and crossed her legs. "Now, Mrs. Youngbeck, tell me about it. What happened?"

"It was terrible, just terrible, the way those boys were hitting that old man. Lady and I were out for our constitutional—we walk two hours every day; gets us out of the house; gives my nephew's wife a chance to clean. . . ." For a moment she was lost in her own concerns, but she shook them off. "Lady loves to chase the squirrels. It's not allowed but. . . ." All at once she remembered she was talking to a police officer. "She's so old she can't possibly catch one. Anyhow, we'd just got to the top of the hill and seen what was going on. I screamed for help, but there wasn't anybody around. Finally I saw the police car, but it was a long way off and they were still beating that poor man. So I turned Lady on them."

"Lady bit one of them?"

"I'm sorry about that, but what else was there to do? Those . . . bad boys wouldn't stop. I had no choice but to sic Lady on them." She leaned over to stroke the weary dog. "Lady chased them. She saved that man's life."

"Weren't you afraid?" Norah asked.

"For myself, you mean? Of course not. Lady wouldn't have let them touch me."

Norah gave the dog a couple of pats. "How good a look did you get at them, Mrs. Youngbeck? Could you describe one or all of them?"

"There were two boys in blue. They had dark hair, nearly black, like yours, dear, but they wore theirs longer. They had thin, pointy faces with not much chin. They looked very much alike; they could be brothers. The other one—the one in red, the one Lady bit—he was a big boy, overweight. He had short, wavy hair, light brown, and strange eyes . . . sort of watery-looking."

"He was the leader," Norah prompted.

"Oh, no, not at all. In fact, he didn't take part in the beating

19

till the very end, not till the little one ordered him to hit the old man. Sometimes, you know, the big ones are the timid ones. They shoot up so suddenly—overnight, it seems; they don't know their own strength; they don't have time to adjust. Sometimes they never do adjust, particularly if they were sickly as children. I'd say that was the case with this boy; he was certainly older than the other two."

Norah felt a chill of apprehension. Mrs. Youngbeck kept referring to the perpetrators as "boys." Probably she would consider Norah, at thirty-three, a "girl." To a woman close to eighty anybody under fifty qualified as young. Still. . . . "How old would you say the 'boys' were?"

"The two in blue—incidentally, one was called Duncan— the brothers, I'd say they were thirteen or fourteen."

Norah gasped. "Are you sure?"

"Oh, absolutely. I used to teach school—junior high. I can tell. The big one, he might be seventeen, even eighteen." She sighed. "Children, just children."

3

"I DON'T KNOW what bothers me more," Norah admitted, blue-gray eyes flashing. "I don't know whether it's that the victims are so old or that the criminals are so young."

Joe sighed. "Both."

"Children not only don't have respect for their elders, they're contemptuous of them. They choose them for victims because they're easy; they can't fight back. Which means that besides being criminals, the children are also cowards. And what does that say about us?" Norah wanted to know.

20

They were at home, dinner over, still at table lingering over coffee. It had been a good meal. Formerly a proficient cook, Norah was becoming a superior one, and Joe, who appreciated good food, was lazily content and just about ready to adjourn to the living room, where he would sneak a little nap behind his newspaper while Norah cleared and put the dishes in the dishwasher. It occurred to Joe that some people might consider his and Norah's homelife uneventful, even dull, and think that they shared few interests. They would be wrong. In fact, Norah and Joe Capretto had a great deal more in common than most married couples—they had their work. Whereas others were separated by their jobs, the Caprettos were joined. The work, woven into their lives, was exciting, demanding of their full capacities. Joe often thought that he and Norah had the same kind of all-consuming passion for police work that an acting couple has for the theater and were as absorbed by it and each other so that there was not time or energy for anything else. These apparently humdrum moments at home were much cherished by both for their very lack of excitement, but tonight was not destined to be one of them. Norah was too worked up. So Joe poured himself another cup of coffee, pushed back his chair, and crossed his legs, prepared to listen.

"Most of these poor old souls are alone in the world; they have no family, no friends, no money." Norah's indignation gathered force. "They're being ripped off by everybody. Their savings, if they have any, are watered down by inflation; the government's threatening cuts in food stamps and in transportation aid—did you know that? Did you hear there might be a reduction in Social Security benefits beginning in July? The nursing homes are a scandal. Most of the old people are just waiting to die. Well, they ought to have the privilege of dying of old age. We ought to be able to assure them of that much."

Joe reached across the dining-room table for her hand. "You're not worrying about your father?"

"Not really, though I must confess Horace Pruitt reminds me of Dad a little—the way he fought for his life, the way he's still fighting."

21

"Has he regained consciousness?"

Norah shook her head. She was silent for so long that Joe thought the subject was closed, at least temporarily.

"We ought to do something!"

"We?"

"Sure, we, the police, who else? That's our job—to protect people. Aren't we coming around to the idea that preventing crime is more efficient than trying to catch the criminal afterward? We have a Crime Prevention Squad."

"Sure we do, but. . . ." Joe didn't finish. She had thought it out. He knew his wife well enough to realize that she had some kind of scheme, was bursting with it. "What do you suggest?"

"We've departmentalized crime. We used to have broad categories—Homicide, Safe and Loft, Vice. Now the distinctions are finer—Homicide and Assault, Narcotics, Organized Crime, Sex Crimes Analysis, Robbery Squad, Emergency Service, Public Morals, Pickpocket Squad. . . . I could go on. So why can't we have a unit devoted to crimes against the elderly?"

"I don't see why we couldn't."

"The unit could patrol the area where the incidence of this type of crime—"

"You've got the regular anticrime and street-crime units doing that," Joe pointed out.

"Sure, sure, but unless they catch the perpetrator in the act, they don't make much effort to trace him."

"You know yourself how little there is to go on in these hit-and-run—"

"There's plenty if you look for it!" Norah insisted, her color high, her eyes bright. "We could work up a profile on the criminal in the same way the Sex Crimes Unit does. Muggings are as subject to solution as any other offense. It's just a matter of taking the trouble."

"And of having the manpower. We didn't have it before," Joe pointed out. "With all the men that have been fired recently and the ax still hanging over the department, we have even less."

"If we had such a squad, it would act as a deterrent, don't you think? And the old people would know that somebody's trying to help. That's important, too."

22

Joe got up, went around to Norah's chair, and kissed her on the temple. "I think it's a great idea."

"You do?"

"Absolutely."

"Then you'll present it?"

"Me? I can't do that."

"But . . . you just said you liked the idea."

"I do."

"So? I don't understand. Why won't you present it to Chief Deland?"

"Because it's not my idea. It's yours, *cara*, and you should be the one to present it. Put it on paper and submit it. I'll help if you want. I'll bet anything you get a favorable response."

"But that could take months," Norah protested.

"You have to go through channels, love. Unless. . . ." Joe frowned. He wanted to help, not only because it meant so much to Norah but because he did basically believe in the idea. "You could talk to Jim Felix. As division commander he could set up a unit within the division. With the kind of pressure he's been getting from the neighborhood citizens' associations, he might just go for it."

"And if it works, if it proves itself, then maybe Chief Deland would expand it to cover the whole city, all the boroughs. . . ."

He started to laugh. "Whoa, slow down, first things first, okay?"

"Oh, Joe." She hugged him. "Why don't we go and talk to Captain Felix together?"

"No, ma'am. This one's yours, all yours. It's your baby."

As soon as he said it, Joe winced. He shouldn't have used that particular cliché. But Norah hadn't caught it. Thank God! His frown eased, so did the knot at the back of his neck. Norah's idea was good; the job needed to be done. He was proud of her for coming up with it. But most of all Joe Capretto was happy to see his wife engrossed in something, anything that distracted her from the loss of their son.

Captain James Felix, commander of the Fourth Division detectives, tilted back in his swivel chair. He was a tall, thin man with wavy red-brown hair and dark green eyes that now roamed over the ceiling tracing the old, familiar cracks and searching for new ones as he considered Sergeant Mulcahaney's suggestion. "Why not?" he mused aloud. "Why shouldn't the old people get some special attention? Everybody else does."

He liked it! Norah could hardly believe it.

"We form the unit to protect a special group, but at the same time we cut down on street crime generally. At the least, it'll get the concerned citizens and the block associations off my back for a while."

Norah held her breath. The reaction was far more favorable than she had dared hope.

Abruptly, Jim Felix leaned forward, and the swivel chair squawked alarmingly. "You do realize that there is such a unit in the Bronx? It's called . . . ah . . . the Senior Citizens Robbery Unit."

"It's mostly advisory, though, isn't it?" Norah countered. "It warns the old people not to open their door to strangers and generally tells them what precautions to take to keep from being victimized. The Street Crimes Unit puts out decoys. What I have in mind is a combination of the two."

Felix leaned his elbows on the desk and looked straight at Norah. He had known her almost as long as Joe, and he had just as high a regard for her abilities. In many ways Norah Mulcahaney Capretto reminded the captain of his wife, Maggie, an actress whose energy and initiative sometimes, often, overcame her caution. "We have to start small," he cautioned. "On a trial basis."

"Yes, sir." Norah swallowed. He was going to do it! Her idea had been accepted.

From the way she sat, spine straight, shoulders squared, chin thrust out, Felix knew he'd let his own enthusiasm show too much. "It'll be a pilot project. The patrol will operate within a limited area. Now, which area would you suggest?" As commander, James Felix knew the neighborhood block by block, by age and by ethnic group; he knew which section it should be.

She answered promptly. "Between Seventy-fourth and Eighty-sixth, from Central Park West to West End Avenue."

"Too big."

"I suppose you could cut the east-west spread to, say, Tenth

24

Avenue, Captain. Most of the single-room-occupancy buildings are on Central Park West and on Broadway, and a lot of
the old people live in them. That residential hotel where we
had the homicide earlier this year, the Westvue, is on Central
Park West and Seventy-fifth. Horace Pruitt, the man who
was mugged in the park, lives on Eighty-fifth. I don't really
see how you can cut north-south and still get a fair sam-
pling."

She had done her homework well and, having had her plan
accepted, was now fighting to give it the best chance for
success. Felix was satisfied. He turned his chair part way
around so he could look at the precinct map on the wall. "I
don't know if I can spare enough men to cover that."

"You only need one shift, Captain."

"How's that?" Felix's high, arched brows lifted a fraction
higher.

"The old people don't go out after dark, not if they can help
it. A lot of the offenders are kids and they're in school till
nearly four. So the prime hours are from four to dark, which
at this time of year is around six."

"Not all offenders are juveniles."

"No, sir, but most of the attacks don't occur till late morning. A special shift from eleven A.M. to seven P.M. should do it."

"All right. How many men?"

"I hadn't thought in actual numbers, Captain."

"Go ahead and think about it."

Lips turned inward, frowning, Norah calculated. The manpower problem was ever present; now, with the mayor's
anticipated budget cuts, the allocation of men was critical. If
she suggested too large a number, the project was dead right
there. She didn't dare suggest too few or it wouldn't work. "I
think it could be done with six. One for decoy and three for
backup, one swingman, and one to take a turn at the phone.
The unit should have a special number, and the public should
be urged to use it. Also, any assault on an elderly person
taking place anywhere in the division should be reported to
the unit."

"No on that, for now. Later on, maybe, but for now I want
the unit to stay within its own limits. Why a three-man
backup?"

25

"Because the perpetrators usually work in pairs, sometimes in gangs."

"Who's going to keep the records, feed the computer, and do the analysis?"

"The head of the unit."

Felix nodded. "Okay. Sounds good, Sergeant. Go ahead."

Norah sat where she was and stared at the captain.

"What's the matter?"

"I'm not sure I understood you correctly, sir."

"I told you to go ahead."

Still Norah didn't move. "You mean you want me to form the unit? You want me to set it up, choose the personnel?"

"Isn't that what you came in for?"

"Captain . . . I came in to present my idea. It never occurred to me that you would . . . that I would . . ."

"Don't you want the job?"

". . . be given command," she finished.

"Who did you have in mind?"

"Nobody. I thought . . . I didn't think. I assumed, naturally, that you'd make the selection."

"Right. I have. You. It's your idea."

"Yes, sir." Somehow she managed to get to her feet. "Thank you, sir. I'll do my best."

"No, not good enough. Make it work, Sergeant."

Norah's eyes met Jim Felix's and held steady. "I will."

"And one more thing, Sergeant Mulcahaney. I want daily reports. In fact, I want to see you in here at the beginning and end of each shift. I want to know exactly what's going on."

Norah left Captain Felix's office in a daze. It wasn't till she was back at her own desk that the full import of what had happened hit her. She was to have her own command! Suddenly she felt like shouting, throwing up her arms, twirling around the squad room between the desks. The thought of the reaction of the other detectives if she were suddenly to dance among them like Carmen among the Spanish soldiers was too much. She started to giggle, but instantly covered her mouth, looking around guiltily. Nobody had noticed; they were all much too busy. It occurred to Norah that she would be making her selection for the team from among these men, subject to the captain's approval, naturally. Then the doubts set in. Could she handle the job? She could. Of course, she could. The captain would not have appointed her if he didn't think so. If he had faith in her, then she should have faith in herself. After all, as both Felix and Joe had pointed out, it was her idea. Her qualms were natural, a result of the unexpectedness of the assignment, that was all. Her own command! What would Joe say? He'd be as elated as she was. She couldn't wait to tell him. She started for his office, but the phone on her desk rang before she was halfway across the room.

"Sergeant Mulcahaney, Homicide," she answered automatically, her mind already grappling with the logistics of the new squad. As soon as the caller identified himself, she set them aside. "Yes, Doctor?"

"You asked me to inform you of any change in Mr. Pruitt's condition."

She knew instantly from the resident's tone what was coming. Horace Pruitt was dead. Thirty-six hours after being assaulted by the three teenagers, without ever having regained consciousness, Horace Pruitt had lost the fight. So now there was no doubt that the case belonged to Homicide. She hung up, gathered the pertinent material, and once again headed for Joe's office. She knocked.

Joe was on the phone talking to a reporter. His back was to the door and he was staring out the window. He sounded relaxed as he parried the questions.

"What can I tell you, Chuck? We had no reason to suppose that the ID was planted. The Stromberg family was satisfied. Now, four weeks later, some man calls up purporting to be Ernest Stromberg and his cousin claims he recognizes the voice. That's no basis for exhumation; you know it as well as I do. Let this alleged Stromberg show himself, and if we get a positive ID from the family, well. . . ." He let it hang.

The reporter's pressure didn't ruffle Joe.

"I haven't the faintest idea why this man should claim to be Stromberg if he isn't, any more than I have any idea how his ID got on somebody else's corpse—if it did," Joe continued. "Certainly we'll reopen the case if the facts warrant. . . . Certainly it'll get my personal attention. . . . How are Leila and the kids? . . . Norah's fine, thanks. . . . Anytime, Chuck, glad to talk to you anytime."

27

Joe hung up. He took a deep breath, held it, then slowly exhaled while continuing to stare thoughtfully out the window. He was head of homicide detectives in the Fourth. Jim Felix had held the post before him, and when Felix was appointed commander of the Fourth Division detectives, he had recommended the man who had worked with him for fifteen years, Lieutenant Joseph Capretto. At first Joe had felt like a juggler who couldn't quite keep all the balls in the air at the same time, but he'd learned. Now he derived a lot of satisfaction in being on top of all current cases.

So what he'd told Chuck Hines, the reporter, was true: He did supervise every homicide in the division, but he didn't second-guess his men. Detective Grodin, however, had already admitted to Joe that he hadn't checked the dental records. Stromberg had been missing for over six months. The private detective hired by the family had traced him to New York and then lost him. When the badly decomposed body, its general specifications matching those of the missing man and bearing his identification, had turned up in an abandoned warehouse, the family accepted that it was Stromberg. Without indication of foul play Grodin hadn't seen any need to pursue the matter. Whether or not Joe would have taken the trouble to check the dental records was beside the point. He'd been in charge for just over a year, and one thing he'd learned was that you couldn't do everything yourself. You chose good men, you trusted them, and then you backed them up. That was the job.

Aware finally that someone was knocking at his door, he called out, "Come. Well, hi, darling. How'd it go? What did Felix think. . . ?" From her expression he gathered that the interview had not gone well, so he amended what he'd been going to say. "What did he think was wrong with the idea?"

Norah frowned. "He didn't think anything was wrong with it. He likes it. It's going to be a pilot unit. I'm to set it up and be in charge."

He couldn't understand why she wasn't more enthusiastic. "That's great, great." Joe had been sure that Felix would go for the plan, and he had even considered the possibility that she might be put in charge, then dismissed it because she had,

28

after all, only recently made sergeant. "That's marvelous. Congratulations, *cara*. I'm proud of you."

"Thanks. What I came in to tell you is that the hospital called. Horace Pruitt is dead."

"Ah," Joe sighed. So that was it. "You knew he was critical," he reminded her.

"He was strong for his age. He fought so hard. . . ."

"Did he regain consciousness?"

"No." She couldn't help but think of her father. Patrick Mulcahaney was not as old as Pruitt, but he wasn't as strong either. He had a physical disability, his left leg having been mangled in an industrial accident years before. For all practical purposes he had overcome it, walking with barely a limp, but if he were to be assaulted . . . would he last even as long as Pruitt?

Joe knew what was on her mind. "How about that witness"—he glanced at the papers she had put on his desk—"Mrs. Youngbeck? I see that she claims she can identify the perpetrators. Is she competent?"

"Absolutely."

"I take it she's been through the mug shots without result?"

The fact that they had a witness who could make identification wasn't of much use if they didn't have any suspects for her to identify. There were no leads either. The way it looked, the only chance they had was to pick up the boys during the commission of another mugging. Though it might seem hit or miss to a civilian, Norah knew from experience that a lot of crimes were solved in just that way. "We'll let it be known that Pruitt didn't talk. That way, whoever did it won't be afraid to go out again. Who knows, maybe you'll get lucky and pick them up. You and the new team."

Norah shook her head. "The fact that they wear those outfits suggests that they work only in the park. Captain Felix has limited our jurisdiction, and the park is not included. I have to agree that it's too large for us to cover effectively."

Joe considered. "I could contact my good buddy Chuck Hines and get him to do a piece for his paper. He could say the park patrol is on the lookout for joggers in those bright outfits. That would make them discard the outfits, and it

29

might also scare them out of the park and into the streets."

"Maybe." Norah wasn't too sanguine.

"And, *cara* . . . why don't you give your father a call? We haven't seen him in a long time. Ask him up for dinner."

4

THE OLD MAN tottered out of Barney's Shamrock Bar and Grill on upper Broadway. He stood on the sidewalk uncertainly, then turned up the collar of his stained raincoat, sizes too big, bent his grizzled head against the light but penetrating drizzle, and started uptown. Weaving from side to side, he lurched toward the gutter, grabbed at a fire hydrant to steady himself, then, overcompensating, lurched in the opposite direction and crashed into a building, bouncing off apparently unharmed. The few pedestrians gave him a wide berth. A young housewife approaching hastily yanked her child out of his path, then stood watching and shaking her head as he made it to Gilhooley's Tavern and staggered inside.

He was out again in a matter of minutes. At Seventy-eighth he turned the corner, heading for Central Park West. He got about a quarter of the way up the block, then, just short of the Mayberry Hotel, a dingy welfare establishment, he leaned against the building for support. Slowly his legs folded under him and he sat on the pavement. Another couple of minutes and his head lolled, his chin dropped to his chest, and his eyes closed.

"Don't you think he's overdoing it?" Norah asked Roy Brennan.

The old man was Officer Ferdie Arenas, black hair streaked with cornstarch, eyes hollowed with a heavy layering of brown

30

greasepaint, acting as decoy for the new unit's first sweep. Norah Mulcahaney and Detective Roy Brennan were following in Norah's car. As Arenas now apparently dozed off, Norah turned the corner and parked.

"When he goes into a bar and comes right out again, it looks like he hasn't got the money to buy a drink," she complained.

"It also looks like he's so far gone the barkeeper refused to serve him. It's a pretty good act, Norah," Brennan assured her.

Good or bad, it didn't matter if nobody was watching, Norah thought, but kept that to herself.

As the special telephone line had not yet been installed, the whole team turned out for this first duty tour. They had started with high hopes. The weather appeared made to order: the early darkness, the rain that kept honest people off the streets. An old man nearly stupefied by drink should have made the perfect target, but Ferdie had been at it for more than three hours and nobody had given him more than a pitying or loathing second look. Norah noted the nondescript black Plymouth turn the corner after her, pass, and proceed up to the far end of the block. That was Detective David Link and Officer Dolly Dollinger. So now the street was sealed at both ends. There was nothing to do but wait.

Sitting beside her, Roy Brennan appeared completely relaxed. Norah, whose jitters had started the night before, almost resented his calm. Of course, he didn't have the personal stake in this that she did. To Roy it was another day's work. And he had no imagination. . . . No, she corrected herself, that wasn't fair: Roy's imperturbability came from experience. He was an old hand; what he lacked in flair he more than made up for in thoroughness and attention to detail. As for caring about the team's success, Roy Brennan wouldn't have joined if he didn't care.

Joe had been surprised that Norah wanted him and had cautioned her on two counts regarding Detective Brennan: one, he was too experienced for the job; two, being her senior by so many years, he might not take orders from her easily. In fact, Roy had once been Norah's direct superior, assigned by Felix to act as a damper to her impulsiveness. Roy had never hesitated to point out flaws in her reasoning, nor had he ever

31

allowed her to take shortcuts in procedure. Yet there had never been any animosity between them. Norah trusted Brennan and wanted him on the team, but on Joe's advice she was careful to leave him an out. Roy Brennan could have turned her down in any number of ways. He could have said he had cases pending that couldn't be passed along, that the special-duty hours wouldn't be convenient, or, being Roy, he could have come right out and told her he wasn't interested. But Roy Brennan, a confirmed bachelor from a blue-collar home, now living alone and used to pleasing himself, had listened while Norah explained the reason behind the unit's formation and then simply said: "Count me in."

It had been a moment of very special satisfaction for Norah. Roy was not only the first man she'd asked, he would also be the senior member of the squad, and so his ready acceptance gave her added confidence in approaching the others. Not that she'd had any real doubt about the others.

David Link, detective first grade, was nearly as enthusiastic as she. David was thirty-four, married, with two children, both boys. He and Norah had started on Homicide North within a couple of months of each other under the supervision of the then Lieutenant Felix and Sergeant Capretto. They were similar in temperament, worked harmoniously, backing each other whenever necessary. Norah expected that David would be her staunchest supporter.

With David at this moment as part of the backup was Officer Ethel Dollinger, nicknamed Dolly. A small, dumpy, cheerful policewoman of twenty-five, with short straight hair cut in bangs and big china-doll eyes peering from beneath them, she was a hard worker. No job was too routine for Dolly. She compiled lists; she ran them down; she canvassed tirelessly. The really tedious research somehow inevitably found its way to Dolly's desk.

"It's like the Rape Squad all over again," she said enthusiastically. Dolly Dollinger had been one of the original members.

"We'll be going out on the street," Norah told her. "We'll be searching out the criminals, baiting them."

"Me, too? I thought you'd want me in the office, keeping the records."

"We'll all take turns at everything. That way we'll each be

32

informed about what's happening and the squad will be better integrated."

"Wow! I'm actually going to get out on the street and do police work! There's only one thing. . . ." Dolly's big brown eyes revealed her anxiety. "How are you going to get me up to look like a feeble old lady?" Norah started to laugh. "I'll go on a diet. I swear I will. This time I mean it."

Ferdie Arenas, now acting as decoy, was the youngest member both in age and in time on the force. He had come from San Juan five years before, and his family were still there. Two sisters worked as maids at the Caribe Hilton; his only brother attended the University of Puerto Rico. They were proud of Ferdie's success up there with the "Continentals"; they considered being a police officer an important job, one that gave them status. They were also grateful for the money Ferdie sent home each month. Arenas was diligent but self-effacing.

"It would be an honor to work for you, Sergeant Mulcahaney." He had grasped Norah's hand when she offered it. "It will be a privilege to help the old people."

That was the regular team. Norah considered it to be well balanced. She had confidence in each member.

The drizzle had become rain and was getting heavy. On the sidewalk Ferdie Arenas was slumped over on one side, apparently passed out. If that didn't attract a mugger, Norah thought, there weren't any muggers around.

Suddenly she sensed a new alertness in her partner. Roy was sitting very straight, watching intently. Following the direction of his gaze, Norah saw a tall, thin male in tight jeans, nail-studded jacket, and chunky platform shoes, highstepping across the street. He wore an Afro hairstyle, but the bluish tinge of the streetlights washed out his complexion so that it was hard to tell whether he was light tan or white. He cast a quick look over his shoulder, then slithered toward the prone figure of Arenas.

He got down on one knee and bent over Ferdie, but the undercover officer didn't move. Nobody in the cars moved. If they announced too soon, the suspect could claim he had been merely trying to give assistance; he had to have the wallet and money actually in his hands and be moving away. The trouble

33

was that he was hunched over Ferdie in such a way that Norah couldn't see what he was doing. So she was startled when Roy flung the car door open and jumped out.

"Police!" he yelled, gun drawn. "Freeze!"

David Link and Dolly were out of their car and running.

It was over in seconds. The prisoner had been read his rights and was on his way to the precinct to be booked by Ferdie and Dolly. The new unit had made its first collar.

Norah was at once elated and disappointed in her own performance. She had been watching the suspect's hands. She realized now that since she couldn't see them, she should have taken her cue from the decoy. As soon as his wallet was lifted, Ferdie Arenas drew up his legs, ready to spring. That was how Roy had known when to move. He had, in effect, taken over. Not that Norah blamed him; it was hardly the moment for consultation. She'd wanted an older, experienced man and, having got him, had better not be sensitive about prerogative.

"It sure didn't need five of us to collar that guy," David complained to Roy.

She couldn't let it pass. "We might have had to deal with a gang."

"In this lousy weather?" David retorted. "Never. All you're going to get in this weather is loners and not many of them. We should have split up for double coverage."

Norah pressed her lips inward nervously. "We'll follow the procedure I set up with the captain."

David raised his eyebrows. "I'm sure the captain expects us to use judgment." Then he added in a conciliatory way, "We've got to show a good record if we want to stay in business."

"We'll stay in business," Norah assured him.

Link shrugged and looked to Brennan.

"She's the boss," Roy said.

The following day, Dolly Dollinger, disguised as an old lady, was accosted by two youths as she came out of the supermarket carrying a bundle of groceries. The bag was knocked out of her arms, her purse seized, and she was thrown to the ground. The perpetrators laughed, but they stopped laughing when the team moved in. As it developed,

34

one of them had a record of two previous arrests for petty theft, and the other had been pulled in on suspicion of rape, though he was later released. They were both white, eighteen and nineteen, respectively, and with enough muscle so that they didn't need little old ladies to knock over.

"Cowards," David muttered, and every member of the unit silently echoed it.

The day after, it was David's turn to be decoy. He wanted to look like a man who had money in his pocket, so he got himself up in a business suit which was out of date but of good quality. He wore a wide-brimmed hat to hide his face and used a cane to help disguise his walk. It was unusually warm for late November, and it seemed to David, as he leaned heavily on his cane, that all the old people in the neighborhood had turned out to sit on the benches on the traffic island in the middle of Broadway. They were squeezed together thigh to thigh and shoulder to shoulder, yet isolated, refusing to acknowledge the body on either side. David had seen similar rows in Queens, the Bronx, on other traffic islands, in housing-project parks, on the sidewalk in front of retirement homes. They sat, raddled faces to the sun, displaced persons in their own hometowns. At the same time, David had been observing a group of four young toughs swaggering aimlessly on the other side of the avenue. They were moving parallel to him, and David thought they were looking him over. He hoped that his apparent lameness would encourage them to select him as a victim. Would they accost him not only in broad daylight but with witnesses abounding? Or should he turn off into a less frequented side street? While he considered, the four crossed over toward him.

David tensed, but the toughs passed him by and continued sauntering along the row of old people like customers examining the merchandise. By common accord they stopped in front of an elderly, shrunken Hasidic Jew in a long black coat and high-crowned black hat, with flowing locks and curly beard. A yank at the beard brought the little man to his feet yelping with pain. They demanded his money, and when he wasn't quick enough in handing it over, they started to slap him and kick him while the old people who had been sitting nearby scattered like frightened birds before a pack of dogs.

35

David threw his cane aside, drew his gun, and announced he was a police officer. But he couldn't fire, not with so many bystanders, and the gang knew it. Alone, David would have been frustrated, but when the team converged, the hoodlums dropped the cowering, whimpering victim, expecting to escape into the crowd. Seeing that someone was actually coming to help, the alienated, terrorized individuals were forged into a single entity. Shoulder to shoulder and thigh to thigh, the old people stood silent, a living barrier against the thugs, determined not to let a single one through.

It was an impasse. For a moment there was silence on the island in the middle of traffic that continued to speed by unheeding. Then one of the youths tried to crash through. In one avenging surge the prey fell on the predators. The old people seized whatever they could—an arm, a leg, a sleeve, a collar, the back of a jacket. They shouted as they dragged the tormentors down and sat on them. Some entwined themselves around their arms and legs like strangling vines on statues. One wizened old woman locked bony fingers into an assailant's long hair, guaranteeing that his first free action would be to get it cut. The mauled youths welcomed the police, relieved to be taken into custody. When all had been removed to the cars, the old people gathered around the officers. Some had tears in their eyes. One woman kissed both Norah and Dolly. Everyone shook hands. It was a moment neither the officers nor civilians would ever forget.

The newspapers latched onto the story and played up the incident. In an age of noninvolvement the way the old folks had come to the aid of the police was news indeed. The old people's unstinted praise for the work of the team turned the spotlight around. The fact that the sergeant heading the unit was a woman, young and attractive at that, didn't hurt either. Sergeant Norah Mulcahaney had her picture in the paper.

The precinct was amused, but little more. Basically, without the trimmings, there wasn't that much to it. The only comment was about Norah's picture. She was complimented, and Joe was teased.

"How does it feel to have a celebrity in the family, Lieutenant?" Detective Augie Baum asked.

36

Joe grinned. "She's still the same simple girl I married."

Captain James Felix decided that this was an opportune moment to announce the formation of the Senior Citizens Squad and its purpose.

Public reaction was immediate and commendatory. The papers cited Felix as compassionate. Representatives of neighborhood associations called on him to express their gratification and support. He was praised for his concern and for his perception in appointing a woman, who was by nature endowed with extra sensitivity to the needs of the elderly and would more readily inspire their confidence. Now the precinct also took note. Reactions were mixed. Norah was congratulated, of course. So was Joe, but with a difference. Those who knew him well probed his feelings with caution. Those who did not asked him right out how he felt. His answer to both was the same.

"I think Norah's doing great. I'm proud of her."

Augie Baum couldn't let it go at that. "Doesn't it bother you?"

Joe replied just as bluntly. "No. Why should it?"

"Well, I mean. . . ." Augie's shrug implied that the reason was obvious. He tried again. "If she were a man, the appointment wouldn't be getting anything like this kind of play from the press."

"Maybe not."

"What do you mean, maybe? That's the truth, Lieutenant, and we both know it. If Norah were a man, the appointment wouldn't rate a paragraph on the back page."

"So?"

"So I'm all for women's rights, equal opportunity, equal pay for equal work, the whole bit. No offense to your wife, you understand, Lieutenant; we all think she's great, a competent officer. . . ."

"She'll be glad to hear that."

"The point is, the thing that started all this commotion . . . it was an ordinary bust. No big deal. Happens every day."

"You miss the point, Baum," Joe contradicted. "It's not this one particular bust that matters, it's the idea behind the squad,

37

which is to show the old people the department cares about them and is trying to protect them. That's what's getting the publicity."

"If you say so, Lieutenant." Baum concealed a sneer.

"Let me ask you something, Baum."

"Yeah, sure, Lieutenant. What?"

"If a man had the command, would *you* be giving it a second thought?" Without waiting for an answer, Joe turned and walked into his office. The exchange with Baum wasn't the first of its kind, and he knew it wouldn't be the last. He was not jealous of his wife's success, but he was getting sick of saying so. He was careful not to slam his door, but it certainly would have relieved him to do it.

After all the attention the squad felt increased pressure to make good. Dissension was banished, and if there was any reservation about the way Norah was running things, she wasn't aware of it. She believed in herself, considered she was doing a good job, and was happy in it. The arrests piled up.

The commissioner sent a note of commendation to Captain Felix. The chief of detectives called Jim Felix to his office.

Louis Deland was a cop's cop—tall, cadaverous, with dark, crepey bags under his eyes. He looked as though he never sat down to a proper meal or ever got his full quota of sleep. Both were true. He had the typical cop reservations about women on the force: They should be matrons, do clerical work, handle juveniles. Louis Deland, however, was a pragmatist: The current of the times was for equality for women, and either you went with the current or you got sucked under. Also, the chief was a fair man, and he had to admit that so far the women had acquitted themselves well. He knew about Sergeant Mulcahaney; she was okay; she possessed a lot of natural instinct for the work.

"I just wonder, Jim, whether the job might not get too big for a woman. I know Mulcahaney's got a fine record, but she hasn't had that many years on the force," Deland reasoned. "Also, I'm not crazy about having her out on the street. I know some of the women are on patrol with a male partner, but that's in a subordinate position."

When assured that the idea for the squad was Sergeant Mulcahaney's, in fact, and not merely for the purposes of

38

publicity, Deland wavered. There was no doubt that Sergeant Mulcahaney was doing a good job. As long as she had plenty of strong, competent backup. . . .

"Keep the unit small like it is now. Don't lay more on her than she can handle. You understand me?"

"Perfectly, sir."

"Good. If the thing really takes off . . . if the momentum continues and we decide to expand . . . well, we can let her handle the administrative work, do some PR—give talks to local groups, like that. She could do some of that right now, as a matter of fact. I'll tell you what else she should do—that's get a special phone number and invite the senior citizens to use it to report anything suspicious. What the hell, you never know —somebody might actually report something useful."

Felix did not pass the chief's remarks on to Norah in full. He edited. He told her that Deland was pleased and that he had suggested the special phone number, but that he, Felix, had not deemed it advisable to inform the chief of detectives that Sergeant Mulcahaney had already put in a request for it.

Norah agreed, happy that they would get the special line at last.

"We ought to send notices of the number to the various neighborhood associations and social clubs," she suggested. "Maybe we could even give little talks about the purpose of the unit at their meetings. I'm sure David or Dolly or either of the others would be willing to go."

"Would you?" Felix asked.

"Sure, anytime."

He nodded gravely. Jim Felix did not deem it advisable to inform her that Chief Deland had already suggested that.

39

5

NORAH WAS worried about her father. Patrick Mulcahaney was behaving oddly. He seldom called and was seldom at home when she called him. When she invited him over for dinner, he made excuses not to come, and when he finally did accept an invitation, he was preoccupied, fidgety, and, it seemed, couldn't wait to get away. It was no different on Thursday night.

They were hockey fans, the three of them, and at this time of year they automatically turned on the TV after dinner to watch the game together. They shouted and exhorted their team as enthusiastically in their living room as they would have done at the game. Only Pat Mulcahaney wasn't joining in. Several times Norah caught him staring off into space when he should have been engrossed in the action on the screen.

He looked well. Now that she was married and no longer saw him every day, Norah was acutely conscious of the physical changes in her father. He had been showing the signs of age markedly—skin becoming crepey, movements tentative, frame shrinking, but lately that process had slowed. In fact, she thought he was putting on weight; certainly his color was better. Also, the drag of his left foot, a barometer of his condition, had been barely noticeable when he arrived.

"What are you up to these days, Dad?" Norah inquired brightly during a commercial.

Patrick Mulcahaney shrugged. "The usual. You know."

And that was out of character. The question should have prodded her father into a minute account of everything going on in his neighborhood.

40

"You look great, really great."

"I feel great. I'm working out again."

"Oh?" Norah frowned. She knew that he still went to O'Flaherty's Gym, but it was a token appearance; he hadn't worked out in at least two years. "You think that's a good idea?"

"Yes, I do."

His tone, if not Joe's look, should have warned her to drop it. She ignored both. "You will be careful not to overdo, won't you, Dad?"

Joe sighed, raising his eyebrows at her.

Norah couldn't stop. "You're not as young as you used to be, you know."

Joe groaned.

"Who is?" Mulcahaney's eyes flashed, but instead of launching into a tirade, he smiled gently. "I'm not into my second childhood yet. Don't fuss, darlin'."

Norah and Joe exchanged glances of disbelief. Well, Norah thought, if her father was so determined to avoid argument, maybe this was the moment to make her announcement. "I've got terrific news."

"Oh?"

"There's a marvelous three-room apartment available in the building. Living room, bedroom, and small kitchen. The super gave me the key. Why don't we go down and take a look at it?"

"You want to move?"

"Not us, Dad—you." She laughed, somewhat hollowly. "It's for you."

"I don't want to move."

Patrick Mulcahaney had steadfastly resisted all offers to come and live with them. He said he didn't want to intrude, and though they wanted him, they did appreciate his consideration. An apartment of his own in their building seemed the solution.

"The old place is too big for you, Dad. Seven rooms for one man! It's ridiculous."

"We want you near us, Pat," Joe said quietly.

Mulcahaney's face softened. Anxious as he had been to see his girl married, he had not favored Joe's courtship. He'd

41

been wrong. He willingly admitted that Joe Capretto was everything he had wanted for Norah. "I appreciate that, but I like it where I am. It's my home. My friends are up there."

"You wouldn't be moving to another city, Dad. You could still see your friends." Norah began the old arguments.

He shook his head. "They wouldn't come down here, not after the first few times. And I'd stop going up there. Sweetheart, I appreciate your concern and Joe's—I really do—but I can look out for myself. You're all involved with the senior citizens thing, but the people you're dealing with are abandoned and helpless. They have nothing to live for. Don't put me in that category. I'm healthy. I've got friends. I've got interests. With the election coming up I'm putting in more and more time at the district club. Above all, I've got you and Joe to call on if I really need help. I'm not going to be easy pickin's for any young hooligan."

Norah was both touched and frightened. "Please, Dad, be careful. If you ever are assaulted, don't resist. It's the worst thing you can do. Let them have what they want. It's only money."

"It's self-respect."

She thought of Horace Pruitt. "It could be your life."

"She's right, Pat," Joe added.

Mulcahaney sighed. "Maybe so."

Meek, meek, her father was too meek! Norah couldn't understand it, and it made her testy. "It wouldn't hurt you just to come down and look at the place."

Mulcahaney reached for her hand. "It wouldn't work, sweetheart. It would be just like moving in with you."

"No, it wouldn't." She was glad that at last an argument was shaping up.

"Yes, it would—exactly. You'd feel you had to have me up for dinner every night, include me when you were entertaining. . . ."

"No, I wouldn't."

"You'd feel guilty if you didn't include me."

"I wouldn't. Okay, okay, we'll make a deal. I promise not to—"

"You'd be running down to cook my meals, to clean my place. Can you promise not to do that?"

42

Norah bit her lip. "I work cheap, Dad."

"Ah, darlin'!" Mulcahaney put his arms around her and held her for a moment. "I'm grateful for what you're trying to do, both of you." He extended a hand to Joe. "It's the sweet, lovin' pair, you are. But let it be."

"I just don't understand it," Norah complained to Joe later as they were getting ready for bed.

"I do. Your father's a proud man, *cara*; he's a fighter, just like you. Giving up his place, whether to move in with us or live downstairs, would be a tacit admission that he's no longer able to look after himself."

"That's silly."

"It's the way he sees it. Remember when your father used to try to get you dates, when he used to bring eligible men up to the house? You resented his trying to run your life."

"It's not the same thing."

"Isn't it? Come on, isn't it?" Joe grinned, pulling her down on the bed. "Here's one old man who wants all the attention you can give him."

As the Senior Citizens Squad settled into an efficient working routine the number of arrests at first increased, then leveled off, then began to drop. Norah found herself doing more and more PR work. She had a full schedule of appearances before community groups. After the first couple of times she got over her stage fright and began to speak easily, even to enjoy it. Her confidence grew on both fronts—as head of the unit and as a lecturer.

At the beginning Joe accompanied his wife whenever possible. He refused to sit on the platform with her because he didn't want to take the spotlight from her, but sitting in the audience night after night got boring, so he started to beg off. Then he didn't know what to do with himself. He had once played handball, but when he tried to revive those games, nobody, single or married, was interested in handball as an entire evening's entertainment. He had never cared for cards, had never been one for hanging around with "the boys," and the entertainments available to him in his bachelor days were not suitable now. There was nothing for Joe to do but sit home

43

and watch television and wait for the sound of his wife's key in the lock.

Norah would return exhilarated, full of the evening's events. She would recount them in detail, and though Joe certainly was interested, he couldn't make himself care about who said what—especially since he didn't know the people. Sensing it, Norah tried to be less exuberant, and that caused constraint between them. Each determined to do better: Joe to show more enthusiasm, Norah less. And each felt a little resentful at having to do it.

With Norah no longer working for Homicide, the Pruitt case had to be passed to someone else. Joe decided to take personal charge. The lab had casts and photos of the footprints on the muddy park slope. Unfortunately the boys had been wearing old sneakers that had left no identifying tread. The piece he'd asked reporter Chuck Hines to do had produced no results. Joe had requested all precincts, particularly the park patrol, to forward any complaint involving a perpetrator wearing a red or blue warm-up outfit, but none came in. He had interviewed Cordelia Youngbeck himself without eliciting anything new. Now that Pruitt was dead, her testimony was crucial. He was satisfied that Mrs. Youngbeck would be able to make positive identification of the youth in red, who had delivered the lethal blow, but they still had to find somebody for her to identify.

With her help a police artist made Identi-Kit portraits of the suspects, and these were circulated. There didn't appear to be anything else that could be done.

Norah had an idea. "Why don't I show the Identi-Kit pictures to my groups when I lecture? Maybe somebody will recognize one of the suspects?"

Joe wasn't too optimistic.

Norah did more than show the drawings. She detailed the case. She described Horace Pruitt's valiant resistance. She made Pruitt the symbol of all elderly victims and enlisted her audience in the army of resistance. "Give a second look at any young man wearing a jogging outfit in those colors," she urged. "If you have any suspicion at all, contact me directly."

She intended, of course, to pass the information on to Joe or

44

whoever happened to be catching for Homicide, but when the call came, Norah had no way of knowing its importance or that it was even connected to the Pruitt case. All she had to go on was a message on her desk that a Mrs. Bertha Tilsit at the West Side Community Center wanted to see her as soon as possible.

She stopped by on her way home. The receptionist informed her that Mrs. Tilsit was a volunteer and was presently working down in the basement. There, in a large bare room, linoleum tiled and lit by fluorescent bulbs, were two long trestle tables with a mound of used clothing in the center of each and about a dozen women working to sort them into stacks. Most of the women were over fifty and physically out of shape. Probably housewives, Norah thought. What they were doing didn't seem exciting to her, but they were chattering cheerfully, apparently having a nice social evening, as well as performing an act of charity. Every head moved in her direction when Norah appeared, and one of the ladies, gray-haired but fresh-faced, with large myopic eyes, left her station and came forward.

"Mrs. Tilsit? I'm Sergeant—"

"Yes, I know you, Sergeant. I was at your lecture two weeks ago. We had quite a conversation afterward. I don't suppose you remember?"

Norah tried, was about to give up, then smiled, "I didn't recall your name, Mrs. Tilsit, but I couldn't forget the lady who baked that delicious gingerbread."

Bertha Tilsit glowed.

"What have you got for me, Mrs. Tilsit?"

Now the lady was all business. Putting her head close to Norah's, she spoke in a low tone, at the same time darting significant glances in all directions to make sure that none of her friends was missing one awesome and delectable moment. They weren't. Nobody was doing any sorting. Nobody was even pretending. Norah was sure that whatever Mrs. Tilsit was about to tell her so confidentially was already known by every woman in that basement room.

"I hope I did right to call, Sergeant. I know how busy you must be; I wouldn't want to bring you out for nothing."

45

"What is it, Mrs. Tilsit?"

"You remember the drawings you showed us of the three suspects in the homicide?"

Norah felt a cold chill move through her. As many times as she got this kind of tip, it was always a surprise. "You've spotted one of them?"

"Oh, no, nothing like that. No, my eyesight isn't too good." Mrs. Tilsit was embarrassed. "In fact, I'm afraid I didn't really see those pictures too well. I've been meaning to get glasses, but. . . ."

Norah hid her disappointment. "Then what did you want to see me about?"

"The suit."

"What suit?"

"You did say one of the suspects was wearing a bright red exercise suit?" She squinted anxiously.

"Oh, yes, that's right."

The eyes widened in relief. "Well, I do believe we have it," she claimed modestly. "You see, people don't usually give anything nearly brand new to a clothing drive. We don't expect it. What we want is good, serviceable, warm garments. What we get is not only out of style, but beyond use. Most times we have to repair it and get it cleaned before we can give it away."

"So?" Norah prodded.

But now that things were going as she'd anticipated, Mrs. Tilsit was in no rush. She was in the spotlight and enjoying it. "We get all kinds of things. You wouldn't believe the unsuitable items people dump on us—satin negligees—I ask you! Evening sandals, bikini bathing suits—junk. Then they want an evaluation so they can take it off their income tax as a charitable deduction!" By now Bertha Tilsit had forgotten that it was all supposed to be confidential; her voice rose and she looked around, inviting support. A dozen heads obliged her by nodding eagerly. "So when I first put my hand on this bright red thing, I thought, now what? Then I saw that it was a sensible garment, warm and nice and in good condition, in fact, practically new. It did have a tear in the leg but that had been sewn." She fixed her gaze on Norah and lowered her

46

voice to a heavy whisper. "Then all of a sudden the reason came to me."

"Where is the suit?" Norah asked.

Mrs. Tilsit led her to a supply closet, reached for a small carton on a low shelf, and put it in Norah's hands. Space was cleared at the end of one of the tables for Norah to set it down and examine the contents. The ladies gathered around, all pretense that they didn't know what was going on abandoned.

"You see, it is perfectly good," Bertha Tilsit reiterated as Norah unfolded the red jacket and held it up. "Hardly worn. Doesn't make sense for anyone to throw it away."

Norah agreed. Examining the pants, she noted that the tear at the left ankle was jagged. Whoever had repaired it wasn't very handy with a needle; nevertheless, the job was adequate and didn't affect the garment's wearability. All labels had been removed.

"Is there any way of knowing who brought this in?"

Mrs. Tilsit's look was one of consultation with the other ladies, all of whom shook their heads. "People just come in and leave their contributions and walk out again," she explained. "Unless they want a tax evaluation, that is. Then they leave a name and address with the bundle. There wasn't any with this."

"Is this the original carton?"

"No, it came wrapped in brown paper."

"I don't suppose you have the paper."

Again Mrs. Tilsit looked to her friends for help, but they couldn't supply it. "I'm sorry."

"Don't be. There was no reason for you to keep it. Was there any other clothing in the bundle?"

Mrs. Tilsit brightened, and the other ladies brightened with her. "Several things."

"Where are they? What did you do with them?"

"I sorted them. I put them in the appropriate piles...." She looked around uncertainly at the various stacks. "They were women's things...." She moved along the table. "There were a couple of heavy woolen skirts, out of style but good quality, and there was a thick cardigan, sort of a rust color." As she talked, she moved, riffling lightly through a stack here and

47

there, becoming more and more agitated. "They'd already been cleaned so I put them on this table," she murmured mostly to herself. "Could I have made a mistake and put them on the other?" Suddenly she pounced. "Here they are! I knew I put them here." She pulled the neatly folded articles she'd described from the bottom of a stack and triumphantly handed them to Norah.

As Mrs. Tilsit had indicated, the articles had been freshly cleaned, and that, Norah thought, could well be all the luck they would need. Yes, the cleaner's tags were still there—in the waistband of each skirt, on the side seam of the sweater.

"You're sure these came in the same bundle as the warm-up suit?"

"Positive, Sergeant."

This time Bertha Tilsit didn't look around for confirmation, but Norah did. Every woman there gave it.

On Thursday night the neighborhood stores would remain open late. Norah called the precinct, but Joe was out. Was there any reason she couldn't do the job herself? She decided there wasn't.

By nine P.M. Norah had located the store where the two skirts and the sweater had been cleaned and had the name of the customer—Mrs. Amy Cotter. The clerk said that a young man—he assumed it was Mrs. Cotter's son—regularly delivered and called for the laundry and cleaning. He didn't know the son's name, but he had no hesitation in identifying the Identi-Kit portrait Norah showed him.

MRS. AMY COTTER opened the door on the chain and peered through the slit.

"Police officer, Mrs. Cotter," Norah announced, and showed her credentials. "May I come in?"

"What is it?"

"I'd like to talk to you."

"If it's about the robbery upstairs, I don't know anything. I wasn't home at the time it happened. I work."

Nowadays there was always a robbery upstairs or downstairs or next door, Norah lamented. "No, ma'am, it's not about the robbery. May I come in?"

Reluctantly Mrs. Cotter slipped the chain.

She was in her early forties, youthfully slim and showing it off in severely tailored slacks and a body-hugging jersey shirt. Her brown hair was liberally streaked with gray and even strands of white, but though she disdained to color it, she had it cut by a master so that with every movement of her head the hair swung freely. The style would have imparted dash to a young face; unfortunately it called attention to the indelible frown of discontent on Amy Cotter's, the puffiness around her eyes, the sullen set of her mouth. The overall impression was one of dissatisfaction and strain. Was she trying to make a statement, to say that one could be over forty and still compete? Or did her job demand this kind of effort?

"I was just paying some bills and straightening out my household accounts." It was not an apology; on the contrary, it was meant to inform the police officer that she was intruding.

The papers spread out on the massive mahogany desk were the only clutter in a rigidly ordered room which reflected the woman and her fortunes. A mixture of old and new—the old, solid and of top quality, indicated she'd been accustomed to the best; the replacements, of lesser grade, that she'd come down in the world, been forced to make compromises. But she still strove for effect: Every ornament was precisely placed, every pillow artfully tossed, and the magazines on the coffee table were arranged for color impact rather than content.

"I'm sorry to disturb you," Norah replied politely.

Mrs. Cotter did not deny she was being disturbed. "What can I do for you, Sergeant?"

Norah wasn't offended. Knowing what was coming, she could only pity the woman. "Is your husband at home?"

"I have no husband."

It was an odd way of putting it, and evidently Mrs. Cotter didn't intend to elucidate. Setting speculation aside, Norah held the carton from the community center out and indicated the coffee table. "May I?" After Mrs. Cotter had cleared space and attempted to minimize the resulting disorder, Norah aggravated it further by opening the box and laying out the contents on the sofa. She began with the two skirts and the sweater. "I believe these belong to you."

"Yes, yes. That is, they did. I gave them to the community clothing drive. What are you doing with them?"

"Did you deliver them yourself?"

"No, my son, Richard, took the bundle over there."

Norah extracted the red warm-up suit. "Does this belong to Richard?"

The frown between Amy Cotter's eyes deepened. "Where did you get that? I didn't throw that out. It's brand new. I just bought it for him."

"You made up the bundle?"

"Certainly."

"Your son must have added the suit to it."

"Why should he do that? I told you it's brand new. You can see for yourself. . . ." She snatched the garments out of Norah's hands as much to examine them herself as to prove her point. "Ah . . . this isn't Richard's. This has a tear in the leg. You see? Obviously it got mixed in by mistake."

"Is Richard at home?"

50

Mrs. Cotter nodded toward the inner hall. "He's in his room, studying."

"Why don't we just ask him if this is his suit?" Norah suggested.

"No, Sergeant, I don't think so. First I want to know what this is about. Why have you brought my things back? And why are you so interested in this warm-up suit?"

"I'd like to speak to your son."

"Is Richard in some kind of trouble?" Amy Cotter's assurance wavered, her voice trembling slightly, but she overcame that immediately. "He can't be. I don't believe it. He's never been in any kind of trouble in his whole life. With all the terrible things that children get into these days, Richard's never caused me one moment's worry. He's a good boy. Whatever it is, Richard had no part in it."

Without comment, Norah showed her the portrait the clerk at the cleaner's had already identified. "Is this your son?"

For a long moment Mrs. Amy Cotter stared at the drawing without any expression at all. She swallowed a couple of times before speaking. "What's that supposed to be?"

"It's a drawing of a suspect in a case of assault and attempted robbery. It was made by a police artist under the direction of a witness to the crime." No use telling her yet that the victim was dead; she had enough to bear. "The drawing has been identified as your son, Richard."

Perspiration broke out on Mrs. Cotter's face. "Who identified it? Who?"

Norah remained silent.

"Well, it's not Richard. It looks like him . . . something like him, but it's not. Whoever said it was is wrong." She cocked her head to one side, pretending to study the portrait. "Actually, now that I look at it again, it's not much like him at all. These drawings—I don't see how anybody can make an identification from them."

Privately, Norah agreed. She never ceased to marvel at a witness' being able to guide the police artist into creating a really good likeness and even more at anyone's being able to make positive identification from it. Nevertheless, it did happen, constantly. The drawings were an important police tool.

51

"According to the witness, the suspect was wearing a red warm-up suit just like this one."

"There must be a thousand of those suits."

"I'm sure there are. That's why I'd like to speak—"

"Assault . . . robbery . . . if you only knew how crazy it is to suspect my boy of such things." The woman laughed, an edge of hysteria in the laughter. "Richard wouldn't hurt a fly. To start with, it's not his nature, and second, he's not physically capable of it. He's not a strong boy. He had polio when he was a child."

That, Norah had not expected, yet hadn't Cordelia Youngbeck when speaking of the eldest and largest of the three boys suggested that he might have been a sickly child? "How long ago?" she asked.

"He was twelve when he was stricken."

"But he's recovered?"

"As much as anybody can from a terrible thing like that," his mother replied guardedly. "He looks fine, but he tires easily. He has periods of extreme debility. He denies it, but I know. I have to keep reminding him that he's not like other boys, that he has to be careful not to overdo."

"Some of our most outstanding athletes were polio victims in childhood," Norah pointed out. "I remember reading about Doris Hart; she took up tennis as therapy for polio and became a champion. There are others who through therapy developed great physical prowess and dexterity—dancers, figure skaters. I think there was even a boxer—"

"And some never got up out of the wheelchair." Amy Cotter gave Norah a patronizing smile. "You do recall Franklin Delano Roosevelt? It depends on the severity of the attack—obviously. In my son's case, strenuous activity was and is out of the question. Richard has been excused from phys ed at school at his doctor's orders."

Did the doctor give the orders at his mother's instigation? Norah wondered. "So Richard takes no physical exercise of any kind? Then why the warm-up suit?"

"I didn't say that. His condition requires a certain amount of controlled physical activity, but nothing strenuous or involving sudden, abrupt exertion."

52

"How old is your son?"

"Seventeen."

While she still held the police artist's drawing in her hand, in Norah's mind another picture was forming—of an overly protected boy, a boy set apart, excluded from the normal play and companionship of other boys, made to feel physically inferior, whether he actually was or not. Again according to Cordelia Youngbeck, the youth in red had been big and strong, but reluctant to use his strength. Could that be because he wasn't accustomed to using it, because he had been told that he was, in fact, a weakling?

"Just exactly what kind of exercise does Richard take?"

"He swims three times a week. He jogs a certain specified distance each day."

"Where?"

"In the park, Sergeant, where else?"

Norah said nothing.

Nevertheless, Amy Cotter knew she'd made an incriminating answer. "Richard is not the only boy who goes jogging in the park, or who wears a red warm-up suit either. I know my son. I know him better than most mothers because I've had to be both mother and father to him. Richard's father abandoned us when he was an infant. He walked out and left us without a cent. I'd never held a job; I hadn't been brought up to work. . . ." She tossed her chicly cut hair, recalling that privileged childhood. "But I went out and found a job. It wasn't much, but it kept Richard and me alive. When he was stricken, I had no medical insurance, but somehow I paid the bills. And when he recovered, I put him in a private school so that he should be in a stress-free situation. I paid for tutoring to enable him to keep up with his age group. Now you come and tell me that he's repaying my sacrifice by slipping away from his exercise group—for which, incidentally, there's an extra charge—and going around assaulting and robbing people. I don't believe it. Why should he do such a thing? I give him everything he needs."

Everything he needs according to your lights, Norah thought, suppressing a sigh.

"Richard doesn't smoke or drink or, God forbid, take

53

drugs. If you think I wouldn't know it if he were doing any of those things, that I wouldn't recognize the signs, you're wrong. I've made it my business to learn what to look for. Richard is a fine boy, and I deeply resent this unfounded accusation."

Norah pitied Amy Cotter and all the parents who were so sure they knew their children and did not, who watched them so carefully for the dreaded signs and then refused to acknowledge them. "I haven't charged him yet, Mrs. Cotter. I just want to talk to him. I could get a warrant. Then the questioning would take place at the precinct. Of course, you could call your lawyer and have him present. Perhaps you'd prefer that?"

Abruptly Amy Cotter sat down and covered her face with her hands. "I don't have a lawyer. I wouldn't know whom to call."

"You could consult the Legal Aid Society. Or the court could appoint someone."

"Oh, God . . . oh, God, how could such a thing happen? What have I done to deserve this? I've sacrificed my whole life for that boy. I could have remarried, I had plenty of chances, but I didn't want Richard to have a stepfather . . . and this is the thanks I get. What will they say at the office? I'll lose my job!"

How many women, personally frustrated, blighted their children's lives in just this way? Norah pondered, yet she felt sorry for Amy Cotter and believed that under the layers of selfishness there was a core of real love. In the crisis she would discover it—unfortunately too late both for her and for the boy. This parent, however, was a fighter and was already emerging from despair to scheme a way out.

"I don't want Richard dragged down to the precinct, Sergeant Mulcahaney. I'm sure that this is all some terrible mistake. So, suppose I let you talk to him here, at home. Nobody would have to know about it, would they?"

"I can't promise that, Mrs. Cotter. I can't promise anything."

"Of course, of course."

But she was counting on just that. Norah could tell, and she had to disabuse her of the false hope. "The situation is quite serious."

"I see." Amy Cotter became very still. Her face, moments before contorted, now was a mask. She got up, started for the hall.

"Mrs. Cotter . . . please, just knock on his door and ask him to come out."

The woman nodded and did exactly as she'd been asked.

Norah could have picked Richard Cotter out of a crowd— the police artist, guided by Cordelia Youngbeck, had drawn that good a likeness. There was the same open face and, albeit somewhat flabby, the same nice, regular features and wavy, light brown hair cut short—at his mother's dictum, no doubt. The portrait could not reveal how big he really was or how awkwardly hunched over he held himself, but a lot of other boys and girls who towered over their schoolmates got into that habit, too. There was something else about Richard Cotter, something not quite right. Norah struggled to define it.

"This lady wants to ask you a few questions, Richard." His mother spoke to him in the soothing tone one might use to someone not very bright.

As Richard Cotter turned obediently from his mother to her, Norah thought she had it—he was a bit retarded, but when she looked into his eyes, she realized she was wrong. Richard Cotter just lacked interest. He had no curiosity and so was deficient in that kinetic energy that should have been consuming a boy of seventeen. "I'm Sergeant Mulcahaney, Richard. I'm a police officer."

He was interested in that, all right, though he tried to hide it. He was frightened, too, and tried to hide that.

"I'm here about an old man who was assaulted in Central Park two weeks ago."

"I don't know anything about it. We didn't go to the park that day."

"What day?"

"The day it happened."

"How do you know which day it was?"

55

"I . . . I read about it. Yes, I read about it in the papers."

"Who's we?"

Richard Cotter was at a loss.

"His exercise group. I explained about that." His mother came to his aid.

Norah waved to her to be silent. Should she read Cotter his rights? The exact moment a witness became a suspect was subject to varied interpretation. If the suspect turned out to be guilty, not having read him his rights could get the case thrown out of court; on the other hand, reading them too soon often frightened a guiltless witness out of divulging valuable information. Norah decided to risk holding off awhile longer.

"Where were you on November twelfth at about three thirty in the afternoon?"

"Home, studying." He glanced quickly at his mother, flushed, and looked away again."

"You're sure?"

"Yes, ma'am."

"What day of the week was that?"

He frowned. "Tuesday. No, Wednesday. I'm not sure."

"If you don't remember what day it was, how can you remember what you were doing?"

"Because I'm always home studying at that time in the afternoon."

"Your mother says you jog in the park in the afternoon."

His color deepened. "No, ma'am. Not anymore. I got excused." He cast another shamed look at his mother. "I wrote a note and signed it with my doctor's name. I hate it; I hate jogging! It's boring."

Later Amy Cotter would undoubtedly give her son a tongue-lashing; for now she was simply relieved.

"So you were at home on the afternoon of the twelfth," Norah continued. "Alone? Did you have any friends over? Did you speak to anyone on the telephone?"

"No, ma'am."

"Did the doorman see you come in?"

"I don't know."

"I'll have to ask him. If he did see you come in, I'll have to ask him whether he saw you go out again. You understand that, Richard?"

"I didn't go out again," he insisted sullenly.

Either it was true, or else he was very sure that he hadn't been seen. "Well, if you've given up jogging for good, I suppose that's why you discarded this very fine outfit." She held up the red jacket and pants.

"I didn't discard any outfit. I wouldn't do that. My mother paid good money for it. My mother works hard for her money."

"This doesn't belong to you?"

"No, ma'am."

"You still have your outfit?"

"Sure."

"See, I told you, I told you!" Amy Cotter could no longer restrain herself. She threw her arms around her son and kissed him. "My baby. My big boy."

"Would you mind showing it to me?" Norah asked.

Norah watched as he disengaged himself and walked out of the room—slowly. Was his left leg dragging? Yes, she thought when he came back, then she turned her attention to the garments he mutely gave her. She examined them closely. Both jacket and pants were in perfect condition—no tear anywhere, not even dirt on the white neckband or on the wrists or at the ankles. In fact, the warm-up suit looked as though it had never been worn.

"Now are you satisfied?" Amy Cotter demanded.

But Norah spoke to the boy. "There were three youths involved in the assault. One of them was bitten on the left leg by a dog. May I see your left leg, Richard?"

He took a step back . . . and winced.

"Richard!" His mother had noticed. "Richard, show her."

"No. I don't want to."

For a moment Amy Cotter stared at her son, then with a sudden lunge she reached down for his pants cuff and jerked up the trouser. The bruise was there, still discolored, swollen, oozing infection.

"Oh, my God."

Norah sighed.

"Richard . . . baby . . . tell her how you got that. Tell her. Explain."

Norah waited. He didn't speak. "You're under arrest. You have the right to remain silent. . . ." Mother and son listened in a daze as she recited the warning based on the Miranda case. "Do you understand these rights as I've explained them to you?"

Cotter nodded. He seemed awed rather than frightened.

"Do you want to say anything?"

He shook his head.

"Do you want to tell me the names of the other two boys who were with you?"

He shook his head energetically.

"Tell her, Richard, please. Tell her. Why should you take all the blame?" his mother pleaded.

Not only did he refuse to look at his mother, he bit his lip as though something might slip out against his will.

"Why are you protecting them? They wouldn't do the same for you. Please, Richard, please, I beg you, for my sake. . . ." Enraged that her appeals were useless, accustomed to taking matters into her own hands, Amy Cotter turned to Norah. "Do you have drawings of the other two like you have of Richard?"

"Yes."

"Show me. Maybe I know them."

"Mom!"

"Show me."

Silently Norah held them out. In her opinion Mrs. Youngbeck had not succeeded as well in guiding the artist in these as she had in the portrait of Richard Cotter. Only a general likeness had been achieved, and she wasn't surprised that Mrs. Cotter was taking a long time studying them. But gradually the frown on her brow eased, and while her son watched anxiously, she cried out, "I do know them!"

"No, no, Mom. . . ."

"Yes, yes. The Vismitin boys. Brett and Duncan Vismitin. I'm sure it's them."

Richard groaned. All color drained out of his pudgy face. If his mother had had any doubts, his reaction dispelled them.

"Those Vismitin kids are lazy good-for-nothings. Juvenile

58

delinquents is what they are," she raged. "You just ask any-body in the neighborhood and they'll tell you."

"Stop, Mom, stop. Don't say any more."

"Why shouldn't I? It's the truth. I told you to stay away from them. They're bad. They got you into this. It's their fault."

"Knock it off, Mom."

His tone startled Amy Cotter. She wasn't accustomed to having her son speak to her like that. "What?"

"I said, knock it off. Nobody got me into anything. I knew exactly what I was doing."

"Don't listen to him," Mrs. Cotter begged Norah. "He doesn't know what he's saying. My poor baby—"

"I'm not a baby. I'm a man. It's about time you admitted that, Mom. And I'm no weakling either. I'm strong, real strong. I knocked that old man down with one punch." He cocked his right fist, took a fighter's stance, and jabbed into the air. "I killed him."

"No . . ." his mother whimpered.

"I killed him. And he wasn't the first one either. There were others, if you want to know. Plenty, plenty of others. I can't even remember how many."

7

IT WAS nearly two A.M. when Joe Capretto emerged from the interrogation room. For four hours he and Norah, two detectives from the DA's Homicide Squad, and a secretary had done little more than listen to Richard Cotter—or Rick, as he insisted on being called. He had been booked in the Pruitt case, and Norah was on her way to the arraignment, which meant she'd be tied up well into the morning. Joe had too much on his mind to go home. He went back into his office.

Of course, Joe Capretto had heard all kinds of confessions: reluctant confessions, extracted by guile, persuasion, or threat; boastful confessions accompanied by vehement justifications; repentant confessions by which the culprit sought relief for his guilt. There were also, as a matter of routine, confessions by the mentally deranged, the "crazies" who turned up to claim credit for every well-publicized atrocity. Certainly it wasn't the first time in Joe's experience that a suspect apprehended on one charge admitted other crimes; that didn't make the confession false. Rick Cotter had spewed out a plethora of details. He had given names, dates, and descriptions of victims and scenes. It was the job of the detectives to challenge the accuracy of such confessions, but their skepticism had acted as a goad to Cotter. He had not merely countered with additional specifics but added to his list of victims as though he would convince them by sheer weight of numbers. By the time they were through, Rick Cotter had confessed to five killings. All five had occurred in one building, the Hotel Westvue, a single-room-occupancy building on Central Park West at Seventy-fifth tenanted principally by welfare clients, prostitutes, and elderly, long-time tenants who couldn't afford to move out. Joe spent the rest of the night at the files reviewing the circumstances of the five deaths for which Rick Cotter claimed responsibility.

The first occurred on March 4 of that year. The victim had been one Phoebe Laifer, female, Caucasian, age seventy-one. Unmarried. Writer of children's books. She'd had a pleasant three-room apartment at the Westvue, having moved in thirty years before, when it was a prestigious address and a gracious place to live. Cause of death: manual strangulation. The motive was assumed to be robbery, but there was no indication of what had been taken, and the apartment was in good order.

The second homicide had taken place on May 3. The victim was Bernice Hoysradt, female, Caucasian, age eighty-two. She had been found bound hand and foot, lying face up on the floor with a rag stuffed into her mouth. Cause of death: suffocation, the rag having been jammed too far down into her throat. Again the motive was assumed to have been rob-

60

bery, and again there was no indication that the apartment had been searched.

In the third instance the victim was a Mrs. Estelle Waggoner, retired vaudevillian and singer, age seventy-seven. Mrs. Waggoner had been in the original American production of *The Merry Widow*. A full-color poster depicting her in her role—wasp-waisted, in velvet and feathers, bejeweled—dominated her living room. She had applied for admission to the Actor's Fund Home in Englewood, New Jersey, had been approved, and was waiting for a vacancy when she was killed. She had been found lying on the floor under the poster that proclaimed the days of her glory—an old lady in a faded housedress and with a knife in her back. Date: July 3.

Rick Cotter had known a great deal about these women—what was in the police files, and more. He knew their histories so well that he named the titles of the books Phoebe Laifer had written. He could describe the photographs on Mrs. Waggoner's walls, the plays they represented, the part she had played, and her costume—down to the black-button boots and the oversized ruby-and-gold brooch prominently displayed on her bosom.

Joe could find no record of a fourth or fifth homicide. Cotter had named names, of course—Isabel Brady and Theodora Zelinsky. In the morning, Joe thought, he'd have to find out what had happened to those women. In the morning. . . . Wearily he raised his head; it was morning. The window was a rectangle of gray light. He leaned back in his chair, closed his eyes for a moment, and when he reopened them, the window was ablaze with a rosy fire. He reached over and switched off the desk lamp. It was six thirty-two.

Five deaths, according to Rick Cotter, all the victims women, all elderly, and all living in the same building. Also, all occurring within a nine-month period—since Lieutenant Joseph Antony Capretto had been appointed commander of the Fourth Homicide Division. It looked bad. In fact, he couldn't imagine how it could be worse.

At the moment, though, what principally concerned Joe were the two unrecorded homicides. Why weren't they in the files? In each case of sudden death in which a physician was

61

not in attendance to file a death certificate, someone from the medical examiner's office examined the body. Joe's hand was on the phone when he realized that the chief, Asa Osterman, was not likely to be in yet. Besides, this wasn't the kind of thing that could be resolved on the telephone. So he would shave, go out for breakfast, and then drive downtown and see Doc in person. It was just after seven when Joe emerged from his office, and already the squad room was filling up. The night watch consisted of a skeleton crew, but the men of the eight-to-four were already coming in. They carried the usual paper sack with a container of coffee and a Danish, but the half-sleepy banter was missing. They were not only early, they were silent and they were alert. They knew. Joe sensed it instantly. The word of Rick Cotter's confession had got around. And its implication.

"Morning, Lieutenant." David Link spoke up loud and clear.

"Morning, sir." Roy Brennan greeted Joe in the same firm tone.

Ferdie Arenas took a step forward.

On special duty with Norah's team, these three weren't due till ten. Their greeting was reinforced by a low murmur from the rest. Normally the kind of confession that Cotter had made, one that cleared several cases from the books, should have been cause for satisfaction, every man on the squad sharing the success. This was an instance of getting out from under the blame. In the final analysis, it was Joe who would bear the responsibility, but his people were there to show their support.

"Lieutenant. . . ."

Detective Gus Schmidt had carried the Laifer case, the manual strangulation. Due for retirement four years ago and eager for it, Schmidt had suddenly lost his wife. Childless, with no outside interests, he had elected to stay on. Formerly a plodding officer, cautious to the point of temerity, he had become one of Joe's most reliable investigators. Joe could not imagine Gus' overlooking evidence, and yet he was obviously worried.

Joe waved him off. "Later, Gus. You, too, Slim." Slim O'Connor, pale, earnest, perpetually harried, had carried case number two: Bernice Hoysradt, suffocation. "I'll see you both later."

Joe knew that as soon as the door closed behind him the talk would erupt. Most of it would be supportive, but there was always someone who got a kick out of the other guy's trouble. He thought he knew more or less how it would go, but, in fact, he would have been surprised.

He was not surprised that Asa Osterman was expecting him.

Osterman was a small, compact man—five three and 120 pounds—sitting behind an oversized desk. Twenty-two years ago he had moved into the chief medical examiner's office, jammed a sofa cushion into the chair, and raised himself to working height. He had a special chair now, but otherwise nothing had changed in the office or the man. Asa's eccentric attire was legend. Today he sported a bright red woolen vest with big gold buttons and a matching red bow tie so wide it hid the collar of his brown striped shirt. Joe didn't smile at him. Few who knew Doc Osterman did. He was an acknowledged authority in forensic medicine; he had single-handedly solved more homicides than any team of detectives; his opinion was eagerly sought and rarely challenged; juries believed him, and his appearance in court virtually guaranteed victory for whichever side he supported. Nevertheless, his bright, sparsely lashed eyes were troubled as he regarded Joe through thick-lensed steel-rimmed glasses.

He tapped the folders in front of him. "Here are the two cases that were not referred to Homicide.

"Case number one," Osterman intoned. "Isabel Brady. Female, Caucasian, so on and so forth . . . here we are. Age sixty-nine. Found in bed. Cause of death: cirrhosis of the liver. Examining physician: Dr. Alan Dubois." He set that aside and picked up the next. "Theodora Zelinsky, so forth and so forth . . . age seventy-five. Found in bed. Cause of death: cardiac arrest. For your information, Lieutenant, she had recently recovered from an attack of pneumonia. Examining physician: Dr. Douglas Pollard." He set that one aside neatly with the first, then folded both hands on the empty blotter in front of him. "Both Dubois and Pollard are good men. They know not only how to do an autopsy, they know how to evaluate the circumstances accompanying a questionable death and how to read the evidence at the scene. There was nothing in either of these two deaths to indicate other than natural causes."

"Cotter says he killed these two women. He says he suffocated them."

Osterman sighed. "Well, it's not impossible. We both know that it's pretty hard to diagnose suffocation as homicidal, particularly when the victim is elderly and weak—as were both Brady, an alcoholic, and Zelinsky, with her heart condition. Of course, if there had been lipstick on the pillow. . . ." The little doctor shrugged. "But there was nothing to arouse suspicion, nothing at all."

"Still, the five of them dying in the same building. . . . I'm not blaming your department, Asa, I'm blaming myself," Joe hastened to assure the medical examiner.

"What for? To start with, two of those deaths were judged natural and you weren't even informed about them. But aside from that, the majority of the tenants in that building are over sixty-five years of age, we'll work out the exact percentage if that will help, and it probably will. So. They're not only old, they are sick, and they've got precious little to live for. So they die. There's nothing suspicious about it."

"Three of them died by violence."

"Two by intent. Your suffocation by gag was clearly an accident."

"Cotter claims intent."

"He also claims five murders. The question here is credibility, isn't it?"

"I appreciate your support, Asa."

"Hell, I'm not supporting you, Lieutenant," the medical examiner cut in testily. "Or alibiing you or anybody else, me and my department included. We deal with an imperfect science. We make judgments based on the known evidence and backed by experience. We could be wrong; nobody's perfect. But on the basis of the present evidence, my opinion is that you've got two separate cases of homicide here. All right, all right, three, with three different MO's."

"What about Cotter's confession?"

Osterman shrugged.

"I can't ignore it."

"Nobody's telling you to ignore it, Joe. What do you usually do with the kooks who come in and confess to the latest sensation?"

"These crimes were not well publicized, Asa." The fact that Joe had to remind him of this most salient fact was a sure indication that Osterman was far more disturbed than he cared to admit. Joe sighed. "I can't figure how Cotter can know so much unless he's guilty."

"So you believe him?"

Joe took a deep breath, held it, then slowly released it. "He certainly took part in the assault on Pruitt. The dog bite on his leg, his getting rid of the warm-up suit—pretty conclusive. Also, we've got a witness. We'll have a lineup this afternoon, and I expect to get a positive ID. As for the rest . . . I don't know."

Asa Osterman had known Joe Capretto for years; he knew the kind of man he was, as well as the kind of officer. He leaned across the desk and spoke sternly. "You want a piece of advice? Don't make a big thing out of this. Don't go around beating your breast and claiming responsibility. Nobody's going to blame you unless you blame yourself."

But Asa Osterman was wrong.

Maybe he had been trying to reassure himself, as well as Joe, but at the very worst he couldn't have expected, nor could he have imagined, the furor that Rick Cotter's confession would cause. Repercussions within the department were inevitable, but public reaction was exacerbated by the press, who knew when they had a good story. Headlines were bold and persistent. Day after day there was no letup. The newspapers could hardly be blamed: The case was fraught with human interest. There was the high school student as self-confessed mass slayer; the loyal, hardworking, self-sacrificing mother; the sordid scene of the crimes, the Hotel Westvue, with its own fascinating history. Feature writers did "pieces" on every aspect. One reporter actually checked into the Westvue for a couple of days, then moved on to other similar single-room-occupancy buildings in mid-Manhattan and wrote his first-hand impressions of the filth and degradation he encountered. It stirred up a lot of indignation—against landlords, against the Social Security and welfare agencies that permitted their clients to live in such squalor, but principally and inevitably the major sensation remained the "mishandling" of the case by the police and the medical examiner's office. No one quite dared to accuse the vaunted chief medical examiner of negligence, certainly not of incompetence—that was unthinkable—but questions were raised about the particular physicians who had judged the last two deaths as natural. There was less reticence in fixing responsibility within the police department. That had to fall on Lieutenant Joseph Capretto. His excellent prior record, the publicity he'd received in breaking past cases made the present lapse puzzling. Joe had rapport with the press, was well liked, but that didn't save him. Even his friend Chuck Hines joined the pack. It was he who recalled the Stromberg case and the goof on identification of the body, which, when Ernest Stromberg presented himself in Joe's office alive and well, had had to be exhumed and remained still unidentified. By insisting that the lieutenant was not directly responsible, Hines clearly implied that Joe didn't keep a sharp enough eye on his men. Could it be that as fine an investigator as he was himself, the lieutenant was not suited for command? Joe bore no grudge because Chuck cited the Stromberg case, but he did think the conclusion was unfair.

As titillating as any aspect of the sensational case was the fact that the officer who arrested Richard Cotter on another charge and was thus unwittingly responsible for breaking the series of hitherto unsolved and unsuspected murders was an attractive woman, Detective Sergeant Norah Mulcahaney, head of the newly formed Senior Citizens Squad. Most intriguing of all, though the point was not belabored, Sergeant Mulcahaney was also Lieutenant Capretto's wife.

Norah was appalled.

The precinct took note and took sides.

"What's Sergeant Mulcahaney got to do with it?" Ferdie Arenas walked over and joined the men clustered around Augie Baum.

Baum shrugged. "She made the bust, didn't she?"

"So?"

"Well, if she hadn't made the bust. . . ." Baum smiled as

66

though the consequences should be evident to anybody with any brains.

"You mean she should have let Cotter go?" Arenas asked.

"No, no, I don't mean that." Baum looked around at his supporters a bit uneasily. "All I'm saying is that it's ironic that she should have made the bust that's causing all this trouble for the lieutenant."

"Yeah, too bad it couldn't have been you."

"What's that supposed to mean?"

"The lieutenant is in no trouble." Agitated, Ferdie Arenas fell into the speech pattern of his native tongue. "Is nobody in trouble except you, *hombre*. You are in big trouble if you do not shut your mouth about the sergeant."

"You going to shut it for me?" Baum demanded. "Go ahead, let's see you try."

Roy Brennan stepped between them. "Okay, that's enough. Knock it off, both of you."

Asa Osterman stuck to his scientific guns. He called in reporters and handed out copies of the statement he was about to make. Perched on his special chair, attired in a bottle-green corduroy jacket and flowing paisley cravat, he summarized the findings of his department in each of the five alleged homicides.

"I have personally reviewed these findings, gentlemen, and they are correct," he concluded, folding his hands in front of him.

Questions exploded. He answered them in his usual dry, brisk manner, wasting no words, but covering the subject precisely. In essence they didn't get any more out of him than they had in the printed statement. They had to be satisfied.

Chief Louis Deland had no choice but to order a study of the handling of the Westvue murders. Public interest decreed all possible speed, and the study was completed in less than two weeks—record time. The report placed on Deland's desk blamed the detectives of the Fourth for failing to spot a pattern. It did not say what that pattern was. It did find a lack of "in-depth investigation."

67

REPORT RAPS COPS ON HOTEL MURDERS, blazed the headlines. "Shake-up of detective unit imminent."

Captain James Felix and Lieutenant Joseph Capretto were summoned to Deland's office. The chief was in his shirt sleeves, jaws clamped on the fourth cigar of the morning, the slimy stubs of the previous three distributed in various ashtrays around the office and throwing off a foul stench. What Chief Deland wanted to know was why the hell the kid hadn't been picked up the first time around. Never mind the two questionable homicides. If Asa said they weren't homicides, that was good enough for Deland. Forget about them. Forget about the death by gag. Why hadn't the kid been picked up and interrogated on the strangulation and the stabbing? He'd been tutored by one of the tenants in the building, hadn't he? He'd been in and out of the Westvue every day, every damn day, right? So how come he'd slipped through their fingers? Deland demanded of Captain Felix while carefully keeping his baleful eyes off Joe.

And, of course, as senior officer and Joe's boss it was officially Felix's responsibility, as well as his problem, to explain. "Cotter's tutoring sessions were finished in January when he took and passed his Regents' exams, Chief. That was two months before the Laifer strangulation. By that time Hughes, the tutor, had moved out, and nobody else mentioned Cotter. We didn't know he existed."

Deland ground down on his cigar. "Lousy luck."

"Cotter's a nice clean-cut young man with short hair and good manners. The old people were crazy about him. None of them ever considered him in connection with the crimes. They used to have him in for cake and coffee after his lessons. He listened to their stories," Felix continued.

"Then he went back and killed them," Deland commented sourly.

"Maybe."

Chief Deland raised his shaggy eyebrows, shifted the cigar. "You got something new? Something that says he didn't?"

"No, sir," Felix admitted regretfully.

"How about the two kids with Cotter in the park? What's their name—Vismitin?"

68

"I interrogated them myself, Chief," Felix replied. "They claim they hardly know Cotter. They ran into him in the park and he invited them to join him in some fun. It was supposed to be a joke." Felix sighed. "You know how hard it is to talk to kids when a juvenile officer is standing by and monitoring every word, but I just got the feeling. . . . Well, I don't like the way it adds up."

Louis Deland recognized a hunch, and he'd been around too long to underestimate a good officer's instincts. He wanted to know the basis, however. "Yeah?"

Felix knew he was being offered a chance and seized it. "Cotter says he killed those people during the commission of a robbery, but there's no evidence he ever stole anything, absolutely none. We haven't found the money, and we haven't found anything he could have spent it on."

"So he did it for kicks."

"But the woman who witnessed the assault in the park claims that Rick Cotter hung back, that he never laid a hand on the old man till the old man had the younger kid by the throat, and even then all he did was pull Pruitt off. If he'd already killed five times, it doesn't figure for him to have been so squeamish."

Deland grunted. "Maybe he knew there was a witness. Maybe he held off because of her."

"Maybe. But what was he doing running around Central Park as part of a gang?" Felix decided the moment was favorable for bringing Joe into the discussion. "Lieutenant Capretto caught that and he's made a pertinent observation." He nodded to Joe to go ahead.

But Joe waited for the chief's permission, which was given somewhat irritably.

"Speak up, Lieutenant. What've you got?"

"Sir, either Cotter's a loner or a groupie. The murders at the Westvue were committed by a loner, in secret, without the need of the kind of reinforcement Cotter got to make him flatten Pruitt. Psychologically, he doesn't figure for the two styles."

Deland was disappointed. "That may be true. But it's not evidence."

"No, sir," Felix agreed. "We've got him nailed on the

assault. Here's a kid who's been treated like a weakling his whole life, always behind in the regular schoolwork, excluded from normal participation in sports and after-school programs with other boys his age. He's been looked down on, and he wants to show that he's got guts and that he's as strong as anybody. So he gets in with two other kids and goes around the park ripping off the old people. I don't think he cared about the money. I think he was just trying to build up his own ego by terrorizing easy victims. Then he gets caught. His mother falls back on the usual alibi that her son is a physical weakling. He just can't take that anymore. He knows he's going to be charged with the old man's murder, so he figures he might as well make a big man out of himself and confesses to everything he can think of."

The cigar in Chief Deland's mouth had gone out. He removed it, staring at it with distaste, but whether for the cigar or the situation the two anxious detectives couldn't tell. "We can certainly look for the defense psychiatrist to take that line." Somewhat more amiably he addressed Joe. "You got any other suspects, Lieutenant?"

"No, sir," Joe had to admit. "We've interrogated the tenants of the Westvue again, but there's a heavy percentage of transients. A lot of the people who were living in the hotel at the time are gone, and they weren't the type to leave a forwarding address. So after eliminating the staff, delivery people, the regular loiterers, we came up empty."

"Too bad. It would have taken some of the pressure off. As it is, we've got to do it another way. Get me?"

Unfortunately they did, and there was nothing for it but to bow their heads to the chief's edict. When they left Deland's office, Jim Felix was in charge of the Westvue investigation and temporarily also head of the Homicide unit, and Joe was transferred to headquarters—also temporarily.

Norah was distraught.

She had been waiting all day to hear the results of the meeting. As the hours passed and Joe didn't call, she became increasingly worried. By dinnertime, when he finally came home and told her about the transfer, she couldn't contain her dismay.

70

"It's not fair. It's just not fair! You should be conducting the investigation."

"I'm biased. It's to my interest to prove Cotter's lying."

"He is!"

"Yes, I do finally believe that, but any evidence I would turn up to support that would be . . . well, let's say it wouldn't be as readily accepted as it will be when Jim Felix turns it up."

Norah sighed.

"Actually, the chief could have brought a man in from another division to replace me; he showed a lot of consideration. Putting Felix in charge leaves the job open and makes it look like my transfer really is temporary."

"I wish I'd never found that damned warm-up suit," Norah muttered.

Joe gave her a weak smile. "It wouldn't have made any difference."

They put their arms around each other and stood for a few moments in the middle of the living room, silently comforting each other. Norah gave him a soft, lingering kiss, then disengaged herself.

"If the circumstances of his arrest had been different. If he hadn't felt compelled to show off to his mother. . . ."

"That, believe me, was inevitable. It was programmed the day Rick's father walked out on the two of them."

"I wish I'd never started the whole senior citizens thing!"

"Okay, that's enough. Do you mind? Please. I've had it. I've really had it with the whole subject." Joe's face darkened and he turned away.

"I'm sorry."

"I don't want to talk about it anymore. I'm home. I want to forget my problems. I just want to have dinner and relax. Okay?"

"Okay, sweetheart. I'm sorry."

"And stop saying you're sorry."

She was hurt, but she didn't say so. "I'll put the vegetables on and we can sit down in about ten minutes."

Having started to unburden himself, Joe couldn't stop. "There's nothing for you to be sorry about. Actually, I'll be

71

glad to move to HQ. At least I won't have to listen to any more remarks."

"What kind of remarks?"

Joe shrugged. "Oh, you know."

"No, I don't."

He looked searchingly at her. "You mean nobody's said anything to you?"

"About what?"

"Forget it. I shouldn't have brought it up."

"Well, you have, so now tell me."

"Oh, some of the men have been making cracks. It doesn't mean anything."

"What kind of cracks?"

He shrugged. "Do I resent your appointment? How do I feel about your getting all that publicity? Who gives the orders at home? Like that. Most of it is good-natured."

"Most of it?"

"Sweetheart, when you start to climb, you're going to run into some jealousy. That's the price."

"Nobody teased me when you were appointed head of Homicide. All I got were congratulations."

"Right. Sure."

"Nobody suggested I might resent your advancement. Nobody asked me if we observed rank at home."

"Typical male chauvinism, right?" Suddenly Joe started to laugh. "Oh, love, love, don't look like that." He put his hand to her square pugnaciously outthrust chin and waggled it gently. "Come on, loosen up. I don't give a damn what anybody thinks of us; it's none of their business. What's really bugging me is the transfer. I know Chief Deland had no choice, still. . . ." He sighed heavily.

"Are you sure you don't mind about my appointment?"

"Wasn't I the one who urged you to go to Felix and present your idea for the squad?"

"Yes. . . ."

"I'm proud of you, *cara*." He looked directly into her eyes. "I have been right from the day you made detective, and I will be on the day you become the first woman police commissioner—at which time I hope you'll appoint me chief of detectives."

72

Norah started to laugh.

"So why don't you put the meat loaf or whatever delicacy you're concocting in the freezer and let's go out to dinner? What do you say we go to Vittorio's? We haven't been there in a long time."

Vittorio's was 'their place.' Joe had courted Norah in the small neighborhood bar and restaurant, and it wasn't difficult to let the memories take over and erase present trouble. Except that when they got home the trouble was there, waiting: The evening's gaiety was hushed; they went to bed silently, lying back to back, each walled in by his own thoughts.

Certainly Joe had meant it when he had insisted that he didn't blame Norah for his transfer, but he hadn't been completely honest about the gossip. It did bother him. It bothered the hell out of him! He knew, however, that taking any counteraction would make matters worse. Without further material to feed it, the gossip would die down. All he had to do was play it cool. And he did—on the surface. Underneath, Joe Capretto smoldered.

As for Norah, though what he said was warmed by his love for her, she was only partially reassured. She knew her husband: He was a proud man, and the needling he was getting was obviously affecting him. It was all because of the Cotter case, she mused. The Cotter case had opened a Pandora's box of afflictions for them all—for Joe, Captain Felix, the whole detective division. If only the confession could be proved false. . . .

Beside her, Joe stirred restlessly.

Should she ask Captain Felix to let her work on the case? It would mean withdrawing from the Senior Citizens Squad, and she would hate that. The unit meant a lot to Norah; she was proud of the work it was doing, but she would gladly give it up to help Joe. On the other hand, how would he feel about it?

"Darling?" she murmured softly. "Joe? Are you asleep?" She put a hand on his shoulder lightly.

He turned over instantly, drew her to him, held her. She never got around to asking the question.

73

8

NORAH MADE her own decision. It was that the best thing she could do for Joe at this point was to do nothing. But staying out of the case wasn't easy. Being Norah, not taking direct action toward solving both the case and her problem at home made her restive. Roy Brennan and David Link wanted to get back to Homicide so they could take part in the Cotter investigation and, of course, she agreed. They made a point of keeping her informed, but getting the news secondhand was galling. When her frustrations seemed just about insupportable, she reminded herself how much worse it must be for Joe. Yet he showed no impatience. He seemed to have adjusted to his new job, claimed he liked the regular hours, appeared normal, but Norah thought he smiled too much, that his jokes were forced, and there were times when he didn't know she was watching that she caught him staring blankly off into space. She kept her thoughts to herself.

In order to spend more time with her husband, Norah cut down on her speaking engagements. When she couldn't get out of a commitment, she made sure to leave as soon as possible—no more social mingling with the audience afterward. Because her mind was only partially on her work and because by mutual consent they didn't discuss the Cotter case, Norah now turned her attention again to her father. On a free afternoon, with Joe on duty, she decided to look in on Patrick Mulcahaney.

As she walked down the hall toward the door of the apartment on Riverside Drive, Norah heard the sound of the vacuum cleaner inside. Yesterday had been Mrs. Sullivan's day; the apartment shouldn't need cleaning again this soon, she thought irritably. That woman was absolutely useless. Norah directed all her frustrations to the aged cleaning woman who had been with Patrick Mulcahaney since Norah's marriage. Her father had no business running the vacuum. I'm going to catch him in the act. He's not going to be able to deny doing Mrs. Sullivan's job for her. He won't have any excuse not to get rid of her, Norah thought as she jabbed the doorbell. The noise of the vacuum stopped. Norah rang again in case he hadn't heard the first time.

The door was opened on the chain, and a dark-haired woman with bright eyes and pink cheeks peered out.

"Who are you?" Norah asked.

"Mrs. Fitzgerald."

"Where's Mrs. Sullivan?"

"Oh, she doesn't work here anymore. She's retired."

That was the only way her father ever would have got somebody new. Well, thank God for small favors. Norah relaxed and smiled. "I'm Norah Capretto. I'm Mr. Mulcahaney's daughter. May I come in?" Accustomed to verifying her identity, she automatically opened her handbag for her ID wallet. "Here. . . ."

Mrs. Fitzgerald waved it aside. "I know who you are. He's spoken of you."

"Well . . . may I come in?"

"Oh. Of course. Yes, please. . . ."

Once inside the vestibule, Norah gave the new cleaning woman a longer appraisal. Perhaps in her late fifties, she was short, plump—in a pleasant way that suited her. Yet her dark hair showed little gray, and her face was fresh, barely lined, rosy as though it had just been scrubbed. In fact, Norah thought she had never in her life seen anyone who looked so shiningly, scrupulously clean. Norah gave her a warmer smile and passed on through to the living room. She stopped at the threshold. The place had never looked like this! It was shining. Every surface polished, the hardware on chest and table drawers glinted; the rug looked as though it had been recently shampooed.

"You do beautiful work, Mrs. Fitzgerald."

The woman's face became rosier still. "Thank you."

"How did my father ever find you? Through an agency?"

75

"No. It was . . . through a friend of his."

"I don't suppose you have any free time?"

"I'm sorry."

"I guess it was too much to expect. Well, don't let me interrupt you. I'll just go and knock on my father's door; he should be waking up. . . ." She started down the inner hall.

"Uh . . . Mrs. Capretto? He's not in. Your father's not at home."

Norah glanced at her watch; it was just going on three. "Isn't he taking his nap? Doesn't he usually take a nap after lunch?"

"I've never known him to."

Norah considered. Her father had always run out when she cleaned house, claimed he didn't want to get dusted with the rest of the furniture. "Well, thanks, Mrs. Fitzgerald. I'll look in at O'Flaherty's Gym."

"Is it important? What you want to see your father about, I mean?"

"Not really. Why? Do you know where he went?"

"Oh, no. I just thought you might like to leave a message."

Norah frowned. "If he should get back before you leave, just say that I came by." As she started for the door, again marveling at the cleanliness and order, Norah became aware of cooking odors. "Have you got something on the stove?"

"I'm making a bit of stew for his dinner."

Her father's favorite. "Do you always fix his dinner before you leave?"

Mrs. Fitzgerald nodded.

"I thought he was putting on weight. Well, that's wonderful of you, Mrs. Fitzgerald. My father's lucky to have you looking after him, and I'm very grateful. It takes some of the worry off me." She sniffed. "Smells delicious."

Norah didn't find her father that afternoon—not at O'Flaherty's Gym nor at Houlihan's Bar.

"It's not just that he wasn't there today," she told Joe, belaboring the point. "It's that he's changed his whole routine, or rather that he doesn't have a routine anymore. I got the same story in both places. He still shows up, but not regularly as he used to. He just drops by the odd time and then he

76

doesn't stay. Now, you know that's not like Dad. He's kept a rigid schedule and not deviated from it in years."

"But they did see him yesterday and he was okay?"

"Yes . . ." she admitted.

Dinner was over, the dishes done, and the hockey game well into an exciting second period. Joe sat comfortably on the sofa, feet up on the coffee table, watching. Norah sat beside him, feet up, too, but she wasn't paying attention to the game.

"I don't understand why he didn't tell me that Mrs. Sullivan had retired and he'd hired somebody new."

"Probably didn't think it was important."

"After the way I've been after him to make a change?"

Joe shrugged. "Maybe he was afraid you wouldn't like Mrs. Fitzgerald either."

"Not like her? She's terrific. You ought to see the place! She's some cook, too."

"So she's probably expensive. Maybe he was afraid you'd say he's paying her too much." Suddenly Joe leaned forward, every bit of his attention on the screen. "Look at that! Look at that pass. . . . Score! Score!" He turned exuberantly to Norah. "You missed it. It was a terrific play. Never mind, here it comes on instant replay."

She looked, not really taking it in.

Joe sighed. "Okay, what's the problem?"

"I don't know. There was something odd. I had the feeling . . . don't laugh, but I had the feeling that Mrs. Fitzgerald knew where Dad had gone and didn't want to tell me."

"Ah. . . ."

"I know, I know . . . it's ridiculous. I think I'll call Dad." She jumped up and went into their bedroom. Joe heard the sound of dialing, there was an interval, then he heard the receiver being returned to its cradle. Norah came back. "He doesn't answer."

"So he's out."

"Where? It's after nine. He doesn't go to the movies. There's this big game on TV. Why isn't he home watching it as we are? And why doesn't he ever call anymore? What's he up to?"

"I suppose he'll tell you when he wants you to know."

"So you agree he's hiding something?"

77

"You've always been very big on the right to privacy, *cara*. I think you ought to grant your father that right. Now will you please stop pacing and let's watch the game."

She sat obediently but continued to mutter. "He's up to something. I recognize the signs."

Joe hid a grin; he'd heard that before—from Norah's father about her.

Then the phone rang, and Norah jumped up and ran. "There he is!"

The cry had been one of relief and exasperation. Joe knew exactly the kind of loving argument that would ensue, how much of a catharsis it would be for both father and daughter, and settled himself for a long wait. But he had barely picked up the action on the screen when he was aware that Norah was back, much too soon, and that she was standing just inside the door, much too quietly.

"Anything wrong?"

"That was David. He called to let us know that Rick Cotter has retracted his confession."

It didn't change the situation with regard either to the investigation or to Joe.

"Bound to happen, sooner or later," was Joe's comment. "Between that mother of his and a lawyer like Billy Benjamin, I'm surprised it took this long."

Norah tried to squeeze something useful out of it. "It prepares the ground. If Captain Felix is able to clear him of even one of the homicides, then there would be strong doubt that he committed any of the others. It would support the retraction."

"Sure."

"If Cotter's confession can be proved false, as he now claims, then there's nothing to tie those homicides at the Westvue together, is there? And if they're not connected, then there was no pattern and you weren't negligent."

"It sounds simple the way you tell it."

"It would help, wouldn't it, if Cotter could be proved innocent of at least one of those murders?"

"Wouldn't hurt. Have you got an idea?"

"If it could be proved that he was somewhere else. . . ."

"That's the first thing I checked. Naturally. Besides, if the

78

kid had an alibi for any one of those times, he would have presented it in support of the retraction. Did David mention anything?"

"No."

"That's it, then." He held out a hand to her and drew her down to the sofa beside him. "Let's forget about it and enjoy the rest of the game."

But Joe could no longer absorb himself in the action on the screen and Norah knew it. He was worried and unhappy and too proud to show it—even to her. Something had to be done.

In fact, Norah did have an idea and a pretty good one, but she hadn't told Joe because she didn't want to get his hopes up. The idea did, in fact, concern a possible alibi. She went to the captain with it.

Felix was at a loss himself. No matter what Doc Osterman said, how he explained it, the press would not let their readers forget that there were five unexplained deaths which had all occurred in the same building. They printed the medical examiner's disclaimers, but they hinted at multiple murder by one killer, and so it was fixed in the mind of the public. The only way to resolve it was to treat each death individually. So Felix had five separate investigations running concurrently, and not a clue had turned up in any one of them. When Norah entered his office, he was disposed to listen—to almost any suggestion.

"What do you have in mind?"

"An alibi for Rick Cotter." Before he could argue against it, Norah continued. "I think he does have an alibi and he doesn't want to use it because it would get someone else in trouble."

Felix considered. "Like the Vismitin brothers?"

"Yes, sir. Rick was very upset when his mother identified them."

"I interrogated those kids myself," Felix reminded her. "I have to say that I wasn't satisfied at the time, so I'm all for giving it another try." He hesitated, green eyes narrowing. "Now that a finding has been made, I suppose you could go over there on your own, without a juvenile officer, but watch your step. . . ."

"Me? Oh, no, not me, Captain. I'd rather not."

79

That surprised Jim Felix, but only for a moment. He hadn't heard any of the talk, but he was sensitive to the atmosphere of his command and he knew that there were crosscurrents regarding the Caprettos.

"Joe doesn't have to know, though I'm sure he wouldn't mind."

"Well. . . ." Certainly Norah wanted to follow up on her own idea. She was opposed in principle to the pass-along system of one detective, in order to avoid overtime, passing on to a man on the next shift that part of his investigation which he had not been able to complete. It was a false economy because the next man didn't have the feel of the situation and had his own work and often couldn't get it done either. Also, the Vismitin boys were already inured to resisting authority. If they were not approached just right . . . if they guessed what was wanted, they might decide to hold out just from sheer rebelliousness. "I'd rather Joe didn't know."

"That's up to you," Felix said, but he had an uneasy feeling that he'd committed a blunder.

IN THE LEXICON of juvenile justice there is no such word as "guilty." There is no charge. The complainant makes a petition. The young respondent, not *defendant*, appears in family court, and a finding is made. A finding had been made against the Vismitin boys, and they were now awaiting placement—a euphemism for sentencing. Before making placement, however, the judge needed the Probation Department's investigation and report (I & R) plus the psychological evaluation. It might take as long as four months before he got them.

According to the probation officer's initial report, which was made immediately after the boys' arrest, the mother was an alcoholic, divorced, currently living with a man not her husband. In the opinion of the neighbors, the man, George Box, seemed to care for Duncan and Brett Vismitin and while he was at home attempted to exert some control over them. But he was a drifter, a heavy drinker himself, and the relationship with the mother was tempestuous. Periodically George Box walked out, was gone for days, even weeks, then turned up again. Mrs. Vismitin had no job, receiving minimal support from her father, reputedly a rich man living in Florida. The consensus among the neighbors was that the quarrels developed when the money ran out and that George Box returned when the next check was due. It was not exactly a healthy environment, but the law does not permit a juvenile to be held in detention more than twenty days while awaiting the final disposition of his case. None of the agencies that might have taken the brothers had vacancies, so although they were accessories to murder, there was no choice for the court but to release Duncan and Brett in their mother's custody—temporarily. Children who were far worse, who presented an actual danger to the community, had been similarly sent back home. So it was to their home that Norah went to look for Duncan and Brett Vismitin. Having read the report, she thought she knew what to expect.

The screaming was audible in the hall. Norah heard it as soon as she stepped out of the elevator.

"You're not going out that door and that's final!" a woman shrilled hysterically. "You'll leave this house over my dead body. You hear me? Over my dead body!"

"Ah, Ma. . . . Come on, Ma." That was one of the boys.

"You march right back into your room and stay there. Go do your homework. Both of you. Go on. Right now."

"We did our homework, Ma." The voices were coming from the Vismitin apartment. This was the other boy, and he was placating.

"If you go out, I'll kill myself. I swear. Yes, I will, I'll kill myself. Then you'll be sorry. You'll be sorry." The woman began to whine, and the whining gave way to deep, convulsive sobbing. "Why can't you stay home with me? Why can't you

81

ever stay home with your mother? I'll buy you that new color TV for your room that you wanted. And I won't drink anymore. That's a promise. Here, here, Brett, take the glass . . . go on, take it and pour it down the sink. Go on."

Norah decided it was as good a moment as any to ring the bell. At its sound, everything inside stopped, or at least was suspended. Norah could feel the wariness. The door was flung open.

"What do you want?"

Leila Vismitin spoke even before she looked to see who was there; used to trouble, she instinctively attacked first. Dark eyes, heavily outlined with black eye pencil, reddened by drink and tears but flashing nonetheless, bloated face coated by a heavy layer of flour-white powder and streaked with the runoff of mascara, coarse black hair mixed with gray and in need of shampooing, vermilion lips pulled back in a snarl, she blocked the entrance defiantly—a pitiful sight. Then her eyes narrowed. "I know you. You were in family court when my boys' case was heard."

"Yes, ma'am. I'm Sergeant Mulcahaney."

"You testified against them."

"No, not against them, Mrs. Vismitin. I testified to the facts that led to the arrest of Rick Cotter."

The woman shrugged, but remained on guard. "So what do you want? What are you doing here?"

"I'd like to talk to the boys."

"Why? What's happened. What's wrong? What've they done?"

"Nothing, nothing, Mrs. Vismitin, believe me. I just need some information."

Relief breached Leila Vismitin's defenses as no threat could have done, and she fell back. Before the woman could collect herself, Norah entered the apartment. Not quickly enough, for the boys had disappeared. Norah looked the place over.

"It's a dump, a real dump." Leila Vismitin deprecated and apologized at the same time. "I do my best, but I can't keep anything nice, not with two growing boys. They knock into everything."

The furniture was cheap and flashy, junk, the kind that fell apart before the payments were completed and wasn't worth

82

repairing. It all seemed neat enough, but Norah had a feeling the housekeeping wouldn't bear close scrutiny. "It seems very comfortable."

"Don't bother to be polite, Sergeant. It's a dump. Don't think I've always lived like this. I know what a nice home is. When I was a girl, we lived on Park Avenue and we had real antiques."

"I'm sure it was lovely."

"Yes, yes, it was." Mrs. Vismitin's voice softened. Her eyes had a glazed, faraway look. "Did you ever hear of the Gardner School?"

"I'm afraid—"

"It was a private school. The best families, the very best, used to send their girls there. That's where I went to school. It used to be on Madison Avenue in the Fifties. I don't remember the exact street, but it was the nicest part of town. What's the use of even trying to have anything decent over here? The West Side is a slum. Lower Slobovia. That's where I'm living now—in Lower Slobovia."

Actually, it was a good neighborhood. The particular block of West Eighty-sixth on which Mrs. Vismitin lived was lined with expensive apartment buildings and town houses. Her building was eminently respectable.

"You ought to see our place in Miami Beach," Leila Vismitin continued. "It's a block from the ocean and it has a heated swimming pool."

"It sounds wonderful."

"Yes, it is. My daddy's always inviting us to go down and stay with him, but we can't. On account of the boys' school, you know." She paused, then added, "We could go in the summer, of course, but it's much too hot."

"Of course."

Having salvaged some of her pride, Leila Vismitin sat down and indicated that Norah should sit, too. "So what do you want to talk to the boys about, Sergeant Mulcahaney?"

"I'd just like to ask them a few questions."

"Have you got the right to do that?"

"I'm not looking to get the boys into any more trouble, but if you would prefer to have your lawyer present. . . ?"

"That shyster from the Legal Aid! He treated them like
83

hoodlums. They're not bad boys. They're high-spirited. They didn't mean to hurt the old man. It was the other kid, Rick; he was the one. He's bad. He's a killer."

Norah hesitated, then decided to be direct. "Rick Cotter has retracted his confession."

Under her white powder Leila Vismitin turned livid. She began to tremble. "Get out. Get out!"

"Please, Mrs. Vismitin. You don't understand. Calm yourself. There's no question of involving your boys with the Westvue murders. I swear it to you. Please, sit down." Norah went to her, took her arm, and tried to lead her back to the sofa.

The woman shook her off. "What do you want?"

"I want to find out anything I can about Richard Cotter."

A cunning look passed over her face. "You mean you want to find out whether he was lying the first time or now."

"Exactly." Mrs. Vismitin was shrewd enough when it came to protecting her own. Good. "I think your boys can help me. I need their help."

"Why should we give it to you? What do we care what happens to Rick Cotter?" The sullen protest was automatic, a cover while she sized up the situation.

Norah let her take her time.

"A probation officer came to see me the other day. I know I didn't make a very good impression on her. I wasn't feeling well."

This was in the nature of a probe, to which Norah's response was, "I'm sorry."

Mrs. Vismitin switched to a self-pitying whine. "I know she'll put in a bad report, and the judge will send my boys to reform school."

"Training school," Norah corrected.

"Same difference."

Norah couldn't argue.

"I know I'm not making the kind of home for them that I should, but it's better than reform school. It's better than any institution. I love my boys, Sergeant Mulcahaney, I do love them, and I promise to do better by them. Don't let them take my boys away from me."

84

It was a blatant appeal for sympathy, but Norah thought that it was sincere. "It's not up to me, Mrs. Vismitin."

"But you could put in a good word. You could tell the judge that the boys cooperated. Wouldn't that count in their favor?"

It would, of course, but there was no way of knowing how much. Why belabor it? Why not simply agree to put in that good word and get whatever information the boys had to give? Norah couldn't. "The court's decision will be based on your ability to provide an emotionally stable home environment." That meant she'd have to give up George Box or marry him—which probably meant he'd give her up, fast. She'd also have to stop drinking.

Leila Vismitin didn't need to have it spelled out. Hands clasped in her lap to stop their shaking, her voice low, she managed a surprising dignity. "I promise."

Norah sighed. "The court will want more than a promise. You'll have to prove you can do it. There might be a probationary period."

"Would I be allowed to keep the boys? During the probation?"

"Well, you have them now."

"Only because they can't find anybody else to take them. That's not good enough. Every time that doorbell rings . . . when you rang just now I thought it was the social worker come to take them away. My heart jumps. I get goose bumps. I can't stand that. I want to know that nobody is going to come and take them away."

"I'm sorry. . . ."

"I don't want my boys in an institution."

"They wouldn't necessarily. . . ." An idea occurred to her. "How about your father? You say he has this big place down in Miami. Would he take the boys temporarily? I'd be willing to recommend that they be placed with their grandfather while you're . . . making your arrangements. I think the court would look favorably on that solution."

When Norah had first seen Leila Vismitin, she had thought the dead white face and black-ringed eyes grotesque. Now, as the tears welled up anew in the bloodshot eyes, the reaching for youth and glamour seemed not ludicrous but pathetic.

85

Maybe the woman sensed Norah's pity because her tears did not fall; instead she pulled herself up and called in a loud, peremptory tone, "Duncan! Brett! Come in here."

The boys appeared with suspicious promptness. So they'd been listening. Well, it would save going back over the same ground. It was both ugly and sad to see the shrewd look of their clear eyes and the wariness on their young faces. Nowadays the seeds of violence were germinating earlier and earlier. Norah sighed. The criminals were getting younger. Was it already too late for these two?

"You're to answer Sergeant Mulcahaney's questions," their mother ordered. "You hear me? You tell her everything she wants to know."

Both boys nodded obediently; they still seemed to have respect for their mother, and that was encouraging. Immediately after Rick Cotter's confession they had been picked up and interrogated by a detective in the presence of a juvenile officer. According to their statement, they had been associated with Rick Cotter only on that one tragic occasion. Because Cotter was the eldest, the natural leader, the Legal Aid lawyer of whom Mrs. Vismitin had such a low opinion had succeeded in getting the boys remanded to their home to await their final placement. Norah knew that if she challenged their statement directly, she would antagonize both the boys and the mother.

"As I understand it, you weren't close friends with Rick Cotter," she began.

"No, ma'am," Duncan replied, and Brett nodded in agreement with his older brother.

"You took swimming practice with him at the Y, but you never had much to do with him."

"He went to a sh—" Duncan caught his mother's eyes and moderated his adjective. "He went to a sissy private school."

"So how come he asked you to join him in the rip-off of the old man? He did ask you, didn't he? It was his idea?"

"Right." Duncan continued as spokesman, and Brett silently supported him. "Like we already said, we were out jogging and he was out jogging and we joined up. Then we saw the old man. Rick said, 'Let's have some fun.' That's all we meant; we only meant to have some fun with the old man."

86

"So it was the first and only time you did anything like that?"

"Oh, yes, ma'am." The look of innocence that shone on Duncan's face was reflected on Brett's.

"How about Rick? Was it the first and only time he'd done anything like that?"

Duncan shrugged.

"You tell the sergeant what she wants to know," Mrs. Vismitin ordered.

"He said he'd done it before, lots of times. He said it was easy. It was his idea . . ." Duncan whined.

"Yet according to an eyewitness, Cotter held back while you and Brett approached Horace Pruitt. He didn't do a thing till you yelled for him to hit Pruitt."

"Sure, I yelled. The old man was on top of me. He was choking me."

"When Rick lifted him off, you yelled, 'Kill him, kill him.' "

"He didn't mean it," his mother interceded. "He didn't mean for Rick to actually hurt the old man."

Norah's attention remained fixed on Duncan. "After Rick got Pruitt off you, you continued to urge him to 'kill, kill him.' "

"It's just a manner of speaking. . . ." The mother's protest was weaker.

"The old man nearly killed me," the boy muttered.

"When the patrol car arrived, you all ran. The officers immediately put out an alarm to all park patrols to be on the lookout for you, but you got away. I can't figure how you did that. I mean, those outfits you were wearing were certainly conspicuous." She looked from one to the other.

Duncan shrugged, but Brett refused to meet her gaze.

"If somehow you could have got rid of the jogging outfits. . . ." Norah frowned as though thinking it out. "You could have hidden in one of the caves in the Ramble, taken off the suits, and then nobody would have given you a second glance. You could have walked out of the park, right past the officers if you wanted."

Both boys remained obdurately silent.

"If that's the way it was, it was smart, real smart. Quick thinking. Resourceful. You know, I have to hand it to Rick Cotter. He fooled the entire park patrol," Norah marveled.

"To tell you the truth, I didn't think he had it in him. I didn't think Rick was that smart."

"He's not. It was my idea," Dunc blurted out.

"Oh?"

"Yeah."

"Hm." Norah appeared unconvinced. "If you say so. What were you wearing under the jogging outfits? It wouldn't have been just underwear; that would have been even more conspicuous. What did you have on?"

"Regular stuff—pants and a shirt," Duncan replied promptly.

"Why?" Norah asked.

Their mother gasped.

"You were fully dressed under those jogging suits because you'd done it before. You'd had to make a run for it other times, and you were ready."

The boys consulted silently.

Duncan took a deep breath. "Okay, so we ripped off a couplea old people. But we never hurt nobody. Never. We didn't hurt the old man. We never touched him, either one of us."

Norah ignored that. "How many times before? Once, twice, five times, ten, more?"

The mother groaned.

"Always in the park or on the streets, too?"

"In the park mostly."

"When?"

"Jeez, I can't remember."

"There were that many, eh?"

Duncan looked down at his feet; Brett turned away.

"How about the first time? Do you remember the first time you terrorized some poor helpless old person? The day, the place, the victim—anything at all about the first time?"

Mrs. Vismitin couldn't stand any more. "You're making them out to be criminals. They're children, just children, playing a prank."

"Not harmless, though, was it?" Norah challenged.

Leila Vismitin flinched. She turned to her older son. "When was the first time? Tell her."

"Last year. Halloween."

"Aren't you a little old for trick or treating?"

Duncan shrugged. "We're small for our age. That's how we got started. There was this one old lady wouldn't give us anything. Called us rowdies and started to shake this cane she had in our faces and yell for the police at the same time. We ran. The patrol car was coming so we hid in an alley and we heard the old lady complain. The thing was she couldn't tell the cops what we looked like because we were wearing these long black robes with hoods that hid our faces. So we dumped the robes in the trash, and then when the cops were gone, we walked right down that same street, past the old lady's window. She looked out straight at us and never knew us. It was cool."

Norah felt the dread break out into goose bumps—it was even uglier than she had feared. "And that was how you got the idea. You substituted jogging outfits for the Halloween costumes. And it was your idea, wasn't it? Not Rick's."

"Okay. Okay, so it was my idea. So what?"

"So I never could figure Rick for the leader, that's all," Norah answered. "Now, that first time, Halloween, it was just you and Brett, right? Rick didn't come in with you till later. *You* recruited *him*, not the other way around. What I still don't get is, what did you need him for?"

"Muscle," Duncan replied promptly.

As Duncan himself had pointed out, the two brothers were small, thin, their appearance far from intimidating. But with Rick Cotter's hulking presence to back them up, it would have been a foolish victim indeed who refused to hand over what they demanded—as foolish as Horace Pruitt. Probably they'd tried it a couple of times on their own and met with resistance. At least they hadn't turned to knives or guns, Norah thought, and then wondered whether Duncan hadn't deliberately avoided using them because he knew that the possession of weapons would clearly take the incidents out of the harmless-prank category. Could he already possess that degree of criminal cunning? He could. Statistics on the youthful offender were becoming daily more horrendous. How could she honestly intercede for these boys? Maybe there was still a chance for Brett, who seemed merely to be following his older brother's lead, but for Duncan? He needed intensive psy-

chological counseling. He wouldn't get it at Spofford, and
a state mental hospital was an open facility from which
his mother might sign him out at any time. Maybe if
the grandfather were willing to pay for private treatment. . . . She might make that part of her plea to the judge.

"When was the first time that Rick took part in these . . . incidents?"

"I don't remember."

"All right, let's see if we can refresh your memory." Norah
took out her notebook and thumbed through the pages till she
found the list of the Westvue murders. "I have some dates
here. . . ."

"I don't remember dates. I didn't keep records," Duncan
sneered.

It was too much for Leila Vismitin. "Thief! Thief! Liar!"
She sprang forward and slapped her older son across the face.
She grabbed him by the shoulders and started to shake him.
"How could you do this to me? How could you? Why? Don't I
give you everything . . . everything? Why do you need to
steal?"

It was in essence exactly what Amy Cotter had demanded
from her son. Two different women reacting with the same
self-pity and lack of understanding. Norah felt sorry for the
children.

Mrs. Vismitin slapped Duncan again, harder. "Answer me."

Duncan's arms were up around his head, shielding himself.

"That's enough, Mrs. Vismitin. Stop. It won't do any good.
Stop it." Norah had to grab her hand and hold it.

"I've done my best for you, but you're bad, bad. Like your
father. You get it from him. You're his son!" She wrenched
herself free from Norah's restraint and flung herself into a
chair and began to sob convulsively.

"That's enough. You'll make yourself sick."

Because Norah had spoken coldly, without sympathy, the
woman moderated her sobbing to an assortment of sighs and
sniffles.

Norah turned back to the boys. "I'm going to read off some
dates, and you'd better try real hard to remember where you
were and what you were doing then. Maybe you don't keep
records, but the police do. We have a computer, and we can

just punch out all the complaints from old people who were bothered in the park or in this neighborhood on the specific dates I'm going to ask you about. I wouldn't be surprised if at least one of them couldn't positively identify the two of you as their assailants."

"You'll go to jail!" their mother shrieked, the powder washed away and her face an ugly mottled red. "Maybe that's where you belong."

"Mrs. Vismitin, if you don't stop yelling, I'm going to have to take the boys down to the precinct and finish questioning them there. Then these other incidents will have to go on their Youth Department cards and the judge will see them when he reviews the case. I doubt very much that he will then be inclined to grant probation in their grandfather's custody."

For the first time Brett spoke and his voice trembled. "Grandpa won't take us. He doesn't want us. He doesn't like us."

Norah waited for a moment. "Is that true?" Brett nodded. She turned to the mother.

"It's just that the boys are so lively. They make him nervous and he snaps at them," she hedged.

"He threw us out," Duncan confessed.

The bitterness of it saddened Norah. "Well, Mrs. Vismitin?"

"He threw *me* out." It was an admission of defeat. "He threw *me* out because of my drinking and . . . other things. It had nothing to do with the boys. He would have kept them. He wanted them. But I refused to let them stay. I thought he'd let me stay so he could keep them. It didn't work."

The boys watched her, wide-eyed, but she wouldn't meet their look.

Norah put the question as gently as she could. "Do you think he's still willing to take them?"

She nodded. "As long as I'm not part of the deal. He doesn't want me. He says I'm no daughter of his." Leila Vismitin bowed her head.

Slowly Duncan Vismitin turned away from his mother. For a moment hate, real hate, distorted his young face, then it was gone. "You going to see to it that we go to Grandpa?" he asked Norah.

"I'll do my best."

91

"So what do you wanna know?"

"I want to know if Rick Cotter was with you on certain dates. He's the one I'm interested in."

"Let's have them. Shoot."

Norah read from her notebook. "January fourth, that was a Monday. It would have been right after your Christmas holiday."

"No, we didn't go out then much. It was too cold."

"All right. How about April third? That was a Wednesday. As I recall, the weather—"

Duncan interrupted. "We have swimming practice on Wednesdays."

"I see. How about July third? No, that was a Wednesday, too. But school was out by then; were you still having swimming practice?"

"No." He glanced at Brett. "I remember that day because we were supposed to go on a picnic for the Fourth. We were going to Reis Park. George was going to rent a car, and we were all going to spend the day together. We were going to swim and play golf—they have a great pitch-and-putt course . . . ." Just the memory of their plans eased the bitterness from his thin young face. But it hardened again almost immediately. "The day before, the third, *she* started drinking —in the morning." He jerked his head toward his mother, but he kept his eyes averted. "So then she and George had a fight and George walked out. So we decided to get ourselves some bread and go to Reis Park on our own—Brett and me."

"So you were in Central Park on July third. Was Rick with you?"

"Yeah, we called him and he met us. But we didn't make out. It was too crowded. Too many people."

"So then what did you do, the three of you?"

"Just hung around." He shrugged.

The shrug said it all, Norah thought, the lack of interest, the disaffection, the emptiness of his life. "For how long?"

"Well, there was going to be this big rock concert over at the Wollman Rink so we went over there and watched them set up for it."

"What time was that?"

"Oh, I guess . . . I don't know, maybe around four or five in

92

the afternoon. Rick didn't show till close to two thirty because he had to do an errand for his mother, and then he had to leave at six to get home for supper."

Duncan sneered, but Norah detected a trace of wistfulness, even envy. "That's it, then," she said. "Thank you, Duncan, Brett, Mrs. Vismitin." The woman, hunched to one side and wrapped in self-pity, made no reply. What would happen after she left? Norah wondered. Probably she'd go back to her bottle, and the boys would go out to their movie or wherever they'd been headed when Norah rang the doorbell. She hated to walk out on this kind of situation, but what could she do? "Mrs. Vismitin?" The woman didn't even raise her head. "I'll keep my promise. I'll do my best." Getting no answer, Norah started out.

"Ma'am. . . ." Duncan caught up with her at the door. "We'd just as soon you didn't . . . speak to the judge, I mean." He glanced over his shoulder at his mother. She wasn't listening, but he lowered his voice anyway. "The thing is, we've changed our minds, Brett and me. We don't want to go and live with Grandpa. Not without Ma."

"You might be sent to a training school."

"Yeah. Well, we'll take our chances."

Norah looked from one to the other. "You're sure?"

They both nodded emphatically.

"If we go live with Grandpa, Ma's gonna be all alone." Duncan turned toward the sorry, sodden hulk. "Who's gonna look after her if we're not around?"

Norah left the Vismitin apartment exhilarated and confident. Naturally she intended to check with the Parks Department to see if a rock group had been booked on July 3 at the Wollman Rink and find out what time they started to set up, but she really didn't have any doubts about Duncan's story. He had good reason to remember the particular day and no reason to lie about it. The important thing was that he vouched for Rick Cotter's whereabouts on the day Estelle Waggoner was stabbed and for the period covering the time of death as approximated in the autopsy report. It was the first step toward vindicating Joe. Norah couldn't wait to see his face when he heard. First she had to find a phone booth

93

and call Captain Felix and ask him to pass on the good news.

Jim Felix's reaction was guarded. The developments were certainly encouraging, but there was still a long road ahead, he warned. He did agree that Joe could use some encouragement.

"Why don't you tell him yourself?" he urged Norah.

"I'd rather not."

"Okay, then, I'll call him. Is he home now?"

"Yes, he is. And thank you, sir, I appreciate this."

Norah hung up and stepped out of the booth, standing for a moment to fill her lungs with the cool, crisp air. She looked up at a crescent moon and a single star competing with the city lights. It had been a good night's work! As far as she was concerned, the Cotter case was cleared and she was out of it. Of course, Rick would have to answer for the death of Horace Pruitt and she'd have to testify at the trial. But she was willing to bet the case wouldn't come to trial. Rick had a smart lawyer who would plea-bargain him into either a token sentence or even a conditional discharge or probation. She bit back the bitterness: The disposition of a case was none of her business. She thought about the Vismitin children instead. Maybe the grandfather could be prevailed on to relent and forgive his daughter and take her in along with the boys. Maybe she could explain the situation to the judge and he might in turn reason with the old man. . . .

That was for tomorrow. Tonight. . . . She glanced at her watch: ten to nine. She'd be home in twenty minutes at the most. By then Joe would have heard from Captain Felix. Tonight was for celebrating.

10

AS SOON AS Joe got home he changed into a pair of comfortable old slacks and a sports shirt, picked through his record collection, and put on the Steber and Tucker recording of *Madama Butterfly*. The yearning, bittersweet music exactly suited his mood. All Norah had said when she called him at the office was that she'd be working late and he should go ahead and eat. She didn't say what she was working on, and he didn't ask. It used to be that she couldn't wait to tell him everything, and then in turn he'd tell her. Of course, shuffling papers downtown, he didn't have much to tell these days. He was sure that it was out of consideration for his feelings, to spare him embarrassment, that Norah had started holding back, and so their garrulous, uninhibited exchanges had turned into a series of cautious evasions and awkward silences. It frightened Joe that outside of their work they had so little else to share.

He wished he had some idea when Norah would get back, but she hadn't said that either—probably because she didn't know. She'd be back when she was through. He had used to take that for granted.

He wandered into the kitchen, lit the oven, turned the thermostat to 350 degrees as instructed, then got the ham-and-cheese casserole out of the freezer. He started to unfold the foil wrapping and stopped. This was one hell of a way to spend Saturday night! If he had to eat alone, it wasn't going to be a frozen dinner. He rewrapped the package, returned it to the freezer, then went back to the bedroom, where he changed into his good brown slacks and tweed jacket. He slammed out of the apartment just as the ominous music of the Bonze filled the room.

On the street he hesitated. Where should he go? Vittorio's was nearby. It was his and Norah's favorite place. The food was excellent, the wine good and cheap; Vittorio always looked after them personally. Also, Joe knew most of the regulars; he wouldn't be eating alone after all.

For those very reasons Vittorio's turned out to be a bad choice. Where was Norah? everybody asked. Would she be joining him later? Aware that he'd been removed from his command, for the move had had plenty of publicity, his friends worked too hard at pretending everything was normal. They were afraid to ask him anything about himself at all. He drank too much wine, got a headache, and left early. Maybe Norah would be home by now and waiting for him. He hurried. The apartment was as he'd left it—lights blazing, record player still going (something wrong with the cutoff switch), and empty. A glance at his watch showed him it was only eight thirty. He couldn't really expect her back this soon. The music jarred his head; he turned it off and tried the television instead. He switched the dial but found nothing to interest him.

Joe wasn't a drinking man, and he'd already had more than his quota of wine. He wasn't the type who enjoys hanging around bars with strangers either. He was too restless for a movie, but he couldn't stay home. He might run over to see his mother. That presented the opposite problem from the one he'd encountered at Vittorio's. Signora Capretto's attitude toward Norah had softened; she had become genuinely fond of her daughter-in-law, but she still disapproved of her continuing to work. With Norah on duty while Joe was free, Signora Emilia would not be able to remain silent. Despite her best intentions, allusions and innuendos would slip out. Joe wasn't up to making the usual defense.

He could go for a walk. A good long walk in the cold air would clear his head. Except that he didn't want to go for a long walk because he didn't want to think.

He could visit his father-in-law. Why not? Initially, Mulcahaney's objections to Joe had been similar to those of Signora Capretto to Norah: He hadn't wanted her to marry a

96

police officer. But they had vanished as hers had. The two men enjoyed each other's company. He'd go and spend a couple of hours with Pat Mulcahaney. At the same time he could try to find out what, if anything, was bugging the old man. Though Joe had tried to set Norah's mind at rest about her father, he did think she had some basis for concern. This was the perfect opportunity to clear it up. Mulcahaney might well confide man to man what he was reluctant to tell his daughter.

It was twenty to nine when Joe left the apartment. At nine he was ringing Mulcahaney's doorbell.

Mulcahaney opened it partway and stared. "Joe."

"Hi, Dad."

"Well, this is a surprise. Where's Norah?"

"Working."

"Oh."

"I was at loose ends. I didn't know what to do with myself. . . . So I took a chance and dropped by."

Mulcahaney didn't move.

Suddenly Joe got the feeling that he wasn't wanted. "If I've come at a bad time . . . if I'm interrupting anything. . . ."

"No, no, of course not. You're always welcome, Joe. Come on in." Mulcahaney opened the door and stood aside.

Definitely the old man was embarrassed. "I should have called first. Listen, Pat, forget it, okay? I'll drop by some other time." Joe pulled back.

Patrick Mulcahaney reached out to put a hand on his arm. "I'm glad you're here. In fact, I've been meaning to ask you to come by. I need your advice."

When she got back and found the apartment dark and empty, the exhilaration oozed out of Norah. Her first thought was that Joe had stepped out for the papers. If that were all, he wouldn't have turned out all the lights. Next she went into the kitchen. Obviously he hadn't eaten at home. Maybe he'd worked late, too. Hand on the phone, she paused; if he wasn't at the office, it would look as though she were checking up on him. She wandered into the bedroom, turned on the lights, and saw the slacks and shirt he wore around the house tossed in a heap on the bed. So he'd been home and gone out again.

97

Could he have got some kind of emergency call? On his present assignment—not likely. Besides, he would have left a note. Probably he hadn't felt like cooking and had gone out to eat. He'd be back soon. Norah took off her pants suit and got into one of her most becoming robes.

It wasn't till she'd combed her hair, freshened her makeup, and sprayed on cologne that it occurred to Norah that Captain Felix had probably not been able to reach Joe. It would be a shame for him to have to wait till morning for the good news. Maybe she could pass it on as having come from Felix? Of course, that meant calling and warning the captain that she'd done that. . . .

An hour passed. Maybe Joe had decided to take a walk after dinner? Maybe he was waiting for the Sunday papers? Sometimes they didn't come till very late; he was probably standing around waiting for the delivery truck.

Another hour went by and Norah was becoming anxious. If he'd gone to see his mother, why hadn't he left a note to say so? Should she call? No, and for the same reason she hadn't called his office—she didn't want it to look as though she were checking up on him. Also, she didn't want to alarm Signora Capretto in case Joe hadn't been there.

What could have happened to him?

Norah was sweating; her hands were like ice.

It was close to twelve thirty when she heard his key in the lock. She jumped up, started for the door, and then, somehow, couldn't move. It was three and a half hours since she'd spoken to Captain Felix and rushed home. It was too bad that after all this waiting she couldn't share the good news with Joe, but never mind, he was home and safe.

"Where've you been?" she demanded.

Joe, who after a bad start had had a pleasant evening with his father-in-law, was taken aback. "I went out."

She tried to take the edge off her tone, tried to make up for the antagonism of the greeting. "I was worried about you. I didn't know what to think."

"What's to think? I went out. You can't expect me to sit home all night waiting for you."

"No, of course not . . . I know that. It's just . . . I've been home since nine o'clock."

"How could I know that?"

"If you'd bothered to call, you would have found out."

He shrugged. "If I'd known you were going to get home that early, I wouldn't have left."

Actually, she could very easily have given him an indication of when she'd be through, but once you started keeping things back. . . . Norah bit her lip. Never again, she promised herself, never again would she get involved in anything that she couldn't share with him. "I'm sorry I snapped. I don't know what came over me. Forgive me?"

"Nothing to forgive, *cara*."

They kissed, but there wasn't much ardor in it.

"So how'd it go?" Joe asked.

"Okay." Having just resolved not to hold anything back in the future, Norah was distressed that she couldn't say any more. "How about you? Did you have a good time?"

"Well . . ." Joe began somewhat evasively, too, then suddenly he grinned. "Yeah, as a matter of fact, I did. I enjoyed myself thoroughly."

"Good, I'm glad." Norah smiled and waited to hear all about it. When it became apparent he wasn't going to say any more, she had to ask. "What did you do?"

"First I went to Vittorio's for dinner."

"That was nice." Actually, she was a little disappointed that he would go there without her.

"Vittorio asked after you. Everybody did. Paul and Isabel invited me to join them. They'd already ordered a bottle of Frascati, and Vittorio insisted on sending over another one. Then Charlie Barnes came in and he had to buy a bottle. . . ."

Why shouldn't he go to Vittorio's? It had been his place long before it became theirs. "It must have turned into quite a party."

"It was still going strong when I left."

"I thought Vittorio closed at eleven."

"Oh, I left before eight thirty. I came home. I thought you might be back. When you weren't, I went out again."

That hurt. "We just missed each other."

"I guess." He grinned even more broadly. "I went to see your father."

"Oh. Oh, darling, that was nice." She didn't know what

99

she'd thought or feared, but the relief was tremendous. "That was a nice thing to do, sweetheart." She was blushing, knew it, and didn't care.

It wasn't till later, much later, after they'd gone to bed, after the lights were out, that she thought to ask.

"How was Dad? How did he seem to you?"

"Fine. Great. Never looked better."

"Did he give you any inkling of what he might be up to?"

Joe hesitated. "I didn't ask." It was the truth as far as it went. He decided that a little spadework on Mulcahaney's behalf was in order. "Whatever it is, it obviously agrees with him. He's very happy."

Norah's grunt indicated she wasn't convinced.

They were happy the following morning, almost as free and easy with each other as they'd been before the strain caused by Rick Cotter's confession. The glow stayed with Norah into midafternoon. At any moment Joe would hear that Cotter was definitely cleared in the Waggoner killing, and then he would call to pass the news on to her. All day she waited for that call. It didn't come.

Maybe the captain had decided to tell Joe in person and had asked him to stop by. Every time the squad-room door opened, Norah looked up expectantly, but it was never Joe. Maybe Felix had decided to pass the news of Cotter's alibi on to the brass first so that he could tell Joe he had his job back. But it wouldn't happen that fast. It would all have to go through channels, would take days at least, and Norah couldn't see Jim Felix not even letting Joe know it was in the works.

So why didn't Joe call?

It was hard to keep her mind on the job. At six, the end of her special tour, she almost went into Felix's office to ask if he had indeed informed Joe of the new developments, but she didn't—and for the same reason that had kept her from calling his office or his mother last night: She was embarrassed. She went home instead. On the way she stopped at the supermarket for the extra-special cut of sirloin Joe liked, got the Bardolino at the liquor store, and on impulse bought a

100

bunch of yellow roses from a street vendor. Still she tarried, looking idly into shop windows, unwilling to admit that she dreaded going home. Finally she reached her own block; there were no more excuses for delay.

Joe was waiting for her. He was sitting on the sofa, slumped forward, elbows on knees, hands covering his face. At the sound of the door opening he looked up. His face was darker than usual, his expression strained.

Still holding the bundles, Norah stood in front of him and stared. When you love someone, you see him with your heart, Norah knew, but it was years, or so it seemed, since Norah Capretto had looked at her husband with her eyes, and she was not only surprised but saddened by what she saw. She hadn't been aware how gray he'd become, nor how the lines in his handsome face had deepened, nor how many new ones there were. She had always thought of Joe as eternally young and vital, but at this moment he looked every one of his forty-five years. Never mind, we all grow old, she chided herself. Norah had seen Joe tired, depressed, but never defeated. Never before.

She dumped the bundles into the armchair. Her instinct was to go and sit beside him and put her arms around him, but something told her not to. "What is it?"

He sighed. "How could you do it?"

"Do what?"

"Sneak behind my back. Make a fool of me in front of everybody—Jim Felix, the whole bureau."

"I didn't do that. I never would. How can you accuse me of such a thing?"

"Norah . . . Norah . . . stop playing games. Be honest. For God's sake, just for once be straight with me."

A hot wave passed over her. Her stomach tightened into a hard knot of pain. "Just exactly what did Felix say to you?"

"How do you know he said anything? How do you know we even talked?"

Norah flushed and bowed her head. She'd given it away. Dumb, dumb. One look at Joe told her there was no use trying to cover up. "I should think you'd be pleased, delighted that Cotter's confession is discredited."

101

"I would be if it had come about any other way."

Oh, God! Norah thought, and the pain in her stomach made her nearly double up.

"Don't blame Felix, he didn't tell me; he didn't need to. I figured it out—all by myself." Joe was bitter. "You may think I'm so vain that I'm afraid of being overshadowed by my wife, but allow me the intelligence of making a couple of very simple inferences. When Felix talked to the Vismitin kids, they claimed they had nothing to do with Rick Cotter except on that one occasion. There was no way he could budge them. I didn't ask Jim Felix how come they reversed themselves, just—when? He said last night. So unless you want to tell me exactly where you were and what you were working on last night. . . ."

"Nobody else knows I interrogated the Vismitin boys. Nobody else knows I had anything to do with it. I specifically requested—"

"You still don't get it, do you?" Joe sighed. "I don't care who knows!" For a Latin Joseph Capretto was a self-contained man; he never shouted, never—not at his men, not at suspects—never raised his voice to Norah. But he was shouting now. "I want them to know. I want everybody to know. I'm not jealous of you, Norah. I'm not jealous of you professionally any more than I'm jealous of any good, intelligent officer. I've told you a hundred times." Then it was over. "But you shouldn't need to be told."

The quiet and bitter addition hurt more than the rest. "I wanted to spare you."

"From what? A few remarks? You think I can't handle a few remarks—most of them good-natured, at that?"

"I'm sorry."

"I know. You always are." He got up, paced to the window, turned. "It so happens I'm proud of you, of your abilities, of your accomplishments. I thought you knew that."

The pain in her stomach eased. "I do."

"No, I don't think so. If you did you wouldn't have asked Felix not to tell anyone that you were working on the case. You would have known that I'd be happy to have you on it. Grateful for any help you might be able to give me to get my job

102

back. Proud of your loyalty. That I'd want everybody to know you were standing behind me."

"Joe . . . please. . . ."

"Okay." Heaving another sigh, he came back and sat down, but he didn't indicate that he wanted Norah to sit beside him. "The trouble is there's a lack of communication between us, always has been, right from the beginning—before we were married and since. When something really important comes up, you don't consult me. I don't know whether it's because you don't think I'm smart enough . . ."

"Oh, no!"

". . . Or don't have enough guts," Joe continued with determination. "But when there's a crisis you just go ahead and act on your own as though I didn't exist. That's not my idea of what being married is all about."

It was true that she'd kept other things from him. Specifically, she was thinking of their adopted son, Mark, and knew that he was on Joe's mind, too. She'd made both decisions—to adopt the child and to relinquish him—without discussing them with Joe. Then and now, she'd meant only to spare him. She'd had no idea that he resented it so much or that he was so deeply hurt. Nor did she have any idea how to make it right again.

She still had her coat on, but she was cold, freezing. "I don't seem to learn, do I? Everything that's happened is my fault."

"I don't know whose fault it is; I wish to God that I did. I do know that this time you've gone too far. You've interfered in my professional life and humiliated me in front of everybody—our friends, every man and woman in the bureau."

"No. . . ."

"By sneaking behind my back you've as good as announced that I can't look after myself, that I'm an incompetent. You haven't left me any pride."

"Oh, darling, don't—"

"I've told you before, plenty of times, that we're not in competition with each other, but you keep behaving as though we are."

"I don't mean to."

"I've been a cop for a long time, much longer than you, and I also hold a higher rank—for the moment, anyhow."

She flushed hotly. He'd never spoken to her like this. It was on the tip of her tongue to retaliate, to protest that he was going too far, then she thought better of it. Trying to defend herself would, at this point, result in charges and counter-charges; bitter things might be said which, though later for-given, would not be forgotten. The relationship could never be the same. "I'm sorry."

"I'm afraid that doesn't help."

Norah caught her breath.

He looked straight at her. "I'm not saying we should call it off—"

"No!"

Doggedly he went on. "I've given it a lot of thought since I spoke to Jim Felix this morning, and I've decided that each of us needs time for personal reexamination. Each of us needs to be alone to decide what he needs and wants from marriage."

Once a teacher had slapped Norah and caught her against the ear. The blow had deafened her temporarily, caused her to be uncertain in her balance and thus disoriented. It was that way now. The color went out of Norah's world. The rosy light of the setting sun that streamed through the west window turned gray. Joe, his dark, sad face blurred, grew smaller and farther away . . . smaller and farther, diminished, as though she were looking at him through the wrong end of a telescope. His lips were moving; he was saying something, but the words, coming from such a long distance, were faint; she could hardly hear the words, but she knew what he was saying.

"I'm moving out."

He said it only once, but the words echoed and reechoed around her, growing louder and louder each time, booming, shattering till she had to put her hands over her ears and shout to drown them out. "No. No, Joe, don't do that."

The sound of her own voice restored her. The reality around her regained its normal shape and tint. "We can work it out."

It had cost Joe a great deal to say those words. "I hope to God we can."

He walked out of the room, and Norah finally sat down. She

104

sat on the edge of the chair into which she'd dumped the groceries for the night's celebration and the bunch of yellow roses.

He came back too quickly and he was carrying a suitcase—evidently it had been packed and ready.

"I'll let you know as soon as I get settled."

She had assumed that he'd be going to his mother's place. That he wasn't was surely a good sign, meant the separation was really temporary. Didn't it? "What are we going to tell the family?"

"The truth. Nobody else has to know if you don't want them to. That's your decision. Of course, I'll have to give the office a number where I can be reached, and I suppose that after a while it will leak out. . . . Meanwhile at least we won't be working out of the same command; that should save some embarrassment."

"You don't think you'll be reassigned?"

He shrugged. "The case is far from solved. You still don't have an idea who the killer could be."

"Killers," Norah corrected.

"Maybe. I'm not so sure as I was."

"What do you mean you're not sure?" Norah cried out, seizing on this as an outlet. "You have three different MO's. . . ."

"I'll grant you the stabbing doesn't fit, but the strangulation and the suffocation are basically variations of the same method. Add the other two—the deaths of Isabel Brady and Theodora Zelinsky. . . ."

"Asa said their deaths were natural."

"He may have changed his mind."

"Asa?" Norah was amazed. The chief medical examiner did not give an opinion lightly; having done so, he did not reverse himself. It was unprecedented. "Why? What's happened?"

"Late this afternoon the ME's office was called to certify an unattended death. The woman was elderly, had died in her bed. Cause of death: suffocation. It's been marked a CUPI."

That was case unknown pending investigation.

11

ORDINARILY THE death of Mrs. Grace Swann wouldn't have given an assistant medical examiner a moment's uncertainty. He would have categorized it as due to natural causes. But Dr. Alan Dubois had given that opinion in the first of the now suspect and much celebrated deaths at the Hotel Westvue, and he decided that this time he would cover himself by calling his chief's attention to the similarity of circumstances. Asa Osterman had in turn notified Jim Felix.

"I'm not drawing inferences, much less conclusions," the chief examiner cautioned in his dry, caustic manner. "I'm not prepared to quote statistics on the number of natural deaths by suffocation of people over sixty-five years of age either. I'll just say that there seems to be a lot of them lately."

"I see."

"I also want to point out to you, Captain, that it's not all that easy for a person to die by suffocation—naturally, that is. The prime requisite obviously is helplessness—an infant in a crib, a very aged person who is also feeble, drunk, an addict—these would be likely victims. Now, this Mrs. Swann was seventy-three but in relatively good health. There was no alcohol in her blood, nor had she ingested any drugs—sleeping pills or sedatives. In any quantity," he qualified.

"I get the picture."

"I'm not sure you do. Homicide by suffocation is even rarer than natural suffocation. We get maybe three cases a year. It's also hellishly hard to prove. Hellishly. It comes as close to the perfect crime as you can get." He paused. "I'd say that the death of Mrs. Swann warrants a second look—as will any other deaths by suffocation that may occur from here on."

God! Felix felt a cold shiver pass through him. Osterman was no alarmist. If he thought there might be more. . . .

"We have two possibilities," the ME continued. "One: that someone read the information we gave out on death by suffocation in the Westvue case and has adopted it for his use—"

Felix interrupted. "That someone having nothing to do with the original crimes."

"Exactly. That's the first possibility. The second is that the killer doesn't need our information or instruction. He's used suffocation as his method before and he will again."

"How would that explain the knifing and the strangulation?"

"Trial and error," Osterman replied. There was a distinct edge of bitterness in his voice. "Trial and error," he repeated, and hung up.

Felix sat for a while tapping the tips of his fingers together while he thought. It was a matter of determining whether or not Mrs. Grace Swann had died a natural death. Careful though Osterman had been not to commit himself, it was obvious that the medical examiner believed she had not. It was not an opinion that the commander of the Fourth Division detectives was inclined to take lightly. Nevertheless, an opinion, even from such an eminent authority, was not enough on which to build an entire sequence for multiple murder. Jim Felix had to see for himself.

Every instinct told Captain James Felix that murder had been committed in the small overcrowded three-room apartment on Eighty-fourth just two blocks from the precinct house. He could smell it, but he couldn't find the physical evidence any more than Asa Osterman had been able to find the medical. There was no sign of forcible entry. There was no indication of a struggle. The empty teacup and the plate with a few cookie crumbs on a fragile table beside the wing chair indicated Mrs. Swann had had a snack. In the bedroom her clothes were neatly laid on a chair, her shoes lined up side by side underneath it. Everything seemed in perfect order.

Mrs. Swann had not been all that small and frail either. The killer, if there was one, would have needed both strength and expertise to subdue her without leaving a mark on her.

107

According to the neighbors and the building staff, Mrs. Swann had few visitors, and these were mostly tenants in the building, people of her own age and limited vigor.

Still, like Doc Osterman, Felix wasn't satisfied. He sensed that he was missing something. It was there, but he wasn't seeing it. Augie Baum had answered the medical examiner's original request for an investigation by Homicide and he hadn't found anything. Of course, Augie was not noted for sensitivity. What was needed here, Felix mused, was someone with a very special kind of . . . empathy.

For the first day or so after Joe moved out, Norah was numb. She went through the motions of living. In many ways the first night was the easiest. She fixed herself something to eat and ate it though she couldn't taste it, then washed up. With the emptiness of the night stretching ahead she cleaned her house; it was her usual therapy, a way of keeping busy without using her mind. Mercifully anesthetized, physically weary, emotionally numb, she went to bed and fell quickly into a heavy, unrestful slumber. The next morning when she awoke alone in the double bed the full impact hit her. She let the tears come. She sobbed till she knew that she had reached the point of self-indulgence and had to stop. She washed her face, got dressed, and went to work well ahead of time because she had nothing else to do.

Still it was hard to immerse herself in the work. Nobody noticed her abstraction except perhaps Dolly Dollinger. In time, the word was bound to get out, and then she'd have to have some answers, at least an attitude. . . . Why? she asked herself suddenly. Why should she bother? She didn't really care what anybody thought or said, not the family and not the people she worked with. She didn't care any more about the gossip over their separation than Joe had about gossip over her promotion. It was a bitter thing to have to admit.

Yet when she was called to Captain Felix's office, she couldn't help but wonder if he'd heard.

"Sit down, Norah."

His face was grave, his green eyes somber. "How's it going with the Senior Citizens Squad?"

That was a surprise. She submitted daily reports; in fact,

108

there was one on his desk right now. "Slow," she replied. "Of course, street crime is always down at this time of year. We'll have to wait for the warm weather before we can claim any credit."

"The unit's done good work. Are you satisfied?"

Another surprise, but also an opportunity. "I'd like to expand the patrol area, and we could use more people—"

"Hold it." Felix grinned wryly. "What I meant was, do you like the work? Really? Do you like being out on the street?"

Captains don't usually ask sergeants if they're happy in their work. "I think the squad has been very well accepted and is fulfilling an important function."

"That wasn't the question. Do you think you're in the right slot?" This time he didn't wait for her answer. "I don't. I don't think you're a street cop or a desk officer either."

Norah tensed. "Has there been a complaint?"

"No, no. If there were, I'd tell you straight out. Actually, I need you on something else."

"Would that be the recent CUPI, the death of Mrs. Grace Swann over on Eighty-fourth?"

Felix nodded.

Norah took a deep breath. "I'd rather not work on that, Captain."

"Because it would be connected with the Westvue?"

"Yes, sir."

"I consider you the officer most qualified for this assignment. I realize that you're personally involved in the outcome, but if you should come to me and tell me that you can't find any indication that Mrs. Swann's death was anything but due to natural causes, I'll accept that."

Norah was deeply affected. What Jim Felix was saying in essence was that he had faith in her integrity as a police officer to rise above personal considerations.

As for Felix, there was more involved than making an assignment. There was the career and efficiency of two good people. He could have given Sergeant Mulcahaney the order without discussion. But he thought it was important for her to take the case and follow wherever it might lead—important for Joe Capretto, too. "You know that I'm your friend just as much as I am Joe's. . . ."

109

He knew! Joe had told him. That hurt, not so much because he'd done it, but because he'd done it so soon. "I don't think he should have discussed our personal problem."

"All we discussed was your feelings about taking on the case—and his."

"Oh." So he hadn't said anything. She flushed. "We've agreed to a temporary separation."

"I didn't know. I'm sorry." Eight years ago—it didn't seem that long, never does when you're happy—Jim Felix and his Maggie had come close to breaking up. They'd survived and he wanted Norah and Joe to survive, too. "As a man married to a very independent, impetuous, and adorable woman, let me say this to you, Norah: Don't underestimate Joe's capacity—either to love you or to understand you."

He had it wrong, Norah thought. The fact was that she'd relied too heavily on Joe's love and on his understanding. The fact was that he didn't love her enough to accept what he couldn't understand in her nature. She couldn't say so, for no matter how good a friend Jim Felix was, he was still commander of the division and not Dear Abby. Also, this was hardly the time or the place for Advice to the Lovelorn.

"I'd rather not leave the Senior Citizens Squad, Captain. I feel as though I'd be turning my back on the old people."

"Did I say you should?"

"I thought . . . the way I understood it. . . ."

"No, no. I wanted to make sure you didn't have too heavy a work load, that's all. Seems to me that your big argument when you came in to present your idea for the unit was that it shouldn't be merely advisory or a decoy apparatus, but investigative, too. You wanted a unit that would see a case through from beginning to final disposition. Right? Have you changed your mind?"

"No, sir."

"The way I see it, both the Swann case and the Westvue case belong within the purview of the Senior Citizens Squad. Don't you agree?"

"Yes, sir."

"You know there's been a lot of pressure to disband these special-interest squads for economy reasons. A squad that's

110

wiped five open cases from the books would certainly be earning its keep."

"I'll do my best, Captain."

"I expect you to get results, Sergeant."

Norah always felt a deep poignancy when handling the effects of someone recently dead. It was a sad irony that inanimate things survived after the person responsible for assembling them and giving them a life of their own was gone. She thought that she had never been more acutely aware of the spirit of the deceased than she was during the examination of Grace Swann's tiny apartment.

It was crammed with mementos of a lifetime. It was furnished with the cumbersome pieces of an earlier, more grandiose, certainly more spacious abode. There was barely space to thread one's way between tables, chairs, settees, cabinets, consoles of Mrs. Swann's past, a past she cherished because she'd had no present. There wasn't any family—husband dead, no children, relatives on both sides gone, too. She did not even have a television set to offer a window on the present. It was as if she had refused to acknowledge what was outside those cluttered rooms. But she had not been able to keep it outside.

She had been found in bed. She might have lain undiscovered for days but for the watch the old people in the building reported they kept on one another. It could have been called a life watch or a life-support system. It was not organized; it was not even openly acknowledged, but it existed and functioned efficiently. It consisted simply in every aged person making sure that every other aged person was accounted for—every day. It was to guard against being stricken and unable to call for help; it guarded against dying and lying undiscovered till putrefaction. On the morning following her death, Grace Swann should have been in the basement laundry room by eleven. She was not. Quick consultation ascertained that no one had seen her that morning or spoken to her on the telephone. At noon Mrs. Ellen Stanton rang her bell. Getting no answer, she summoned the superintendent and convinced him that he should get the passkey and go

111

inside. Carefully the two of them picked their way through the obstacle course of the living room and entered the bedroom.

It seemed to Norah as she now followed in their steps that it would be extremely unlikely for anyone in a hurry to get in and out without knocking over some knickknack or at least disturbing the precise position of a chair or table. After the shock of what he and Mrs. Stanton had seen, the super, Timothy Losey, was understandably vague as to whether two of the battery of silver-framed photographs on the Jacobean sideboard had been lying face down when they entered. He couldn't swear that either he or Mrs. Stanton mightn't inadvertently have brushed against them. Any one of the procession of people who had been in and out of the apartment since—officers, technicians, medical personnel—might have done so.

Norah noted that there was a tea set on the delicate piecrust table consisting of a small silver tray, pot, creamer, and sugar bowl. The cup was fine china with the dried stain of the tea plainly visible. It struck Norah as odd that Mrs. Swann, who kept everything in such impeccable order, had not washed up before going to bed. She put that small discrepancy at the back of her mind and continued on to the bedroom.

The big tester bed took up most of the space. The pillows which were the apparent cause of suffocation had been tossed aside by Mr. Losey when he discovered the old lady and turned her over to try to revive her. The bed covers had been thrown back when the attendants removed the body. Otherwise, Norah assumed, the scene had not been disturbed. Mrs. Swann's clothes—bra, full slip, old-fashioned corset, which to Norah's modern eyes looked like an armature, and a pair of opaque serviceable old lady's lisle hose—were neatly draped on a chair in a corner. Norah frowned. Where was her robe? It wasn't on the chair or at the foot of the bed. And how about slippers? There should have been slippers nearby in case she had to get up at night. Norah got out the official photos; no robe or slippers appeared. She looked in the closet and discovered a faded blue quilted nylon robe hanging on a hook and fuzzy slippers tucked in the pocket of a shoe bag attached to the inside of the closet door. The management apparently provided adequate heat, and since Grace Swann's nightgown

112

had been flannel, high-necked and long-sleeved, maybe she hadn't needed a robe. But slippers? There was no wall-to-wall carpeting, only a couple of throw rugs, and the floor had to be cold in between. Besides, Mrs. Swann was not the type to go padding about barefoot and then tuck her dirty feet into a clean bed. There was something else. . . . Narrowing her eyes, Norah went over her own bedtime routine. Wash face, brush teeth, put on nightgown and robe, comb hair, and then . . . open window. That was the very last thing; Joe used to do it—now she did. Of course, Mrs. Swann's window was shut now, but in the pictures? Shut.

Timothy Losey, whose rosy chubbiness combined with snow-white hair made him look ageless, replied readily and with every indication of sincere concern. No, ma'am, he hadn't noticed whether the window was open or shut, but he hadn't touched it. Besides using the telephone to call the police, he hadn't touched a thing, not a single thing—he knew enough for that, Sergeant! Seen enough crime shows on TV, Norah thought, and supposed she should be grateful. Since neither the patrol officers nor any of the official personnel who came after them would close the window till the photographs had been taken, it followed that the window had not been open.

Of course, Norah mused, having thanked and dismissed Losey, there were women who did not open their window at night or put their slippers under the bed. She went back to the closet. She took the faded blue robe off the hook and found another nightgown underneath. There might also be some women who put on a fresh nightgown without depositing the soiled one in the laundry hamper. For one woman to vary from the norm in each of these things seemed to Norah highly suspect. If she could find some evidence of another person's presence in the apartment on the afternoon or night of Grace Swann's death, then she would accept that the victim had been manually suffocated, carried to the bedroom, undressed, and put into her bed.

She went back to the living room. The unwashed tea things were as much out of character as the used nightgown left hanging in the closet. She turned abruptly away and went into the narrow kitchen. Its neatness and cleanliness seemed to

113

support her idea, urging her to follow it up. There was nothing on the drainboard, but maybe. . . . Norah stepped on the garbage can's treadle, the lid went up, she peered inside: a broken teacup and about half a dozen perfectly good butter cookies. She reached in and retrieved the broken cup and the cookies.

She had thought it odd that Grace Swann should bring out the silver service to brew herself a solitary cup of tea.

Norah canvassed the building. No one had any idea whom Grace Swann might have been entertaining. The last person to see her on the afternoon of her death was the doorman, Valentine Scharf. He was thin, straight, stiff, and elegant as a walking stick, sporting a small mustache and slickly plastered-down hair with a suspicious redness at the black roots.

"I saw her when she came in from her grocery shopping, Sergeant. And of course she was down here in the lobby earlier waiting for her mail with the rest of them. They're all hanging around waiting at this time of the month."

"Oh?"

"Sure. For their checks. Their Social Security checks. That's what most of them live on." He said it sadly and with a touch of contempt.

Norah stared at him. The Social Security checks. Blessed Mary be praised, the Social Security checks!

"But. . . ." She frowned, eager and yet reluctant to commit herself to his lead. "Don't most of them have their checks mailed to their banks?" Congress, she recalled, had recently enacted a law whereby Social Security benefits could be sent to the bank and deposited to the client's account. The purpose was to avoid delay, loss, or theft. She had assumed everyone would rush to take advantage of the new system. Her father had. Of course most old people were not like her father; they were set in their ways, mistrusted banks, would want the assurance of seeing that government envelope with their name on it, of holding the precious piece of green cardboard in their own hands. "Wouldn't that be a lot more convenient?" she asked.

The doorman shrugged. "All I know is that on the third of

every month half the building is down in this lobby waiting for the mailman."

She had been rummaging through her handbag for her notebook, and now as her fingers closed on it, a new wave of excitement coursed through her. Now she knew what it was about the date of Mrs. Swann's death that had been nagging at her. She flipped through the pages—yes, here. Grace Swann died on Thursday, April 3. Wednesday, April 3, exactly one year ago was the date of Isabel Brady's death—of cirrhosis of the liver. Coincidence? Not when you noted the other dates: May 3, Bernice Hoysradt—suffocation; June 3, Theodora Zelinsky; July 3, Estelle Waggoner.

"The third," she muttered. "The third . . . every time. . . ."

"Yes, ma'am, right on the button," the doorman agreed. "It may not be much but it comes regular. Unless the third's a holiday or a Sunday, naturally, when there's no mail delivery. Then the checks come on the fourth."

Phoebe Laifer had been strangled on March 4. According to the calendar at the front of Norah's notebook, March 3 had been a Sunday.

"And let me tell you, ma'am, it's a real hardship when those checks are even one day late. Some of the old people go hungry." Valentine continued with the same superior attitude as before.

The pattern was glaringly obvious—once you knew. Before even noting the dates, however, certainly before deducing a motive from them, you had to suspect that the deaths were not natural. Therein lay the killer's cleverness. Even Doc Osterman with his years of forensic experience hadn't caught on.

"Was Mrs. Swann entirely dependent on her Social Security allotment?" Norah wanted to know. The doorman was hardly the final authority, but he seemed to be a shrewd observer.

"She was down here every month waiting like the rest of them. As soon as the check came, she went out and loaded up on the groceries like the rest of them." He took a step closer to Norah and lowered his voice. "They spend the money as soon as it comes in. The first part of the month they eat real good, pay their bills, get caught up—then they hang on till the next check." His face sagged. He stroked his mustache. For a moment he looked as defeated as those he had been belittling. "I pray to God every night to keep me on my feet and able to work because no matter how much you put by it's not going to be enough. What with inflation, taxes, the rip-offs, you've just got no control on your future anymore. No control."

That was the reason for the stiff posture, the dyed hair, the youthful mustache. Norah decided Valentine Scharf was afraid. He was afraid of old age. And Norah couldn't blame him.

"Mrs. Swann and the others go right out the same day and cash their checks?"

"Not the same day, the same minute."

There had been no cash in Mrs. Swann's purse or anywhere else in her apartment. No money in the other women's purses or their apartments. "What time is the mail usually delivered?"

"Between two and three in the afternoon."

"That late?"

Barely time to get to the bank before closing, Norah thought. Not that it mattered; banks don't cash checks unless one is a depositor and has a large enough balance to cover the amount. Contrary to their advertising, banks are not in business to do favors. Besides, if those people had wanted to deal with a bank, they would have had their checks mailed there directly. No, they would get cash at the supermarket or at one of the local merchants. Still, all those people wanting cash at the same time. . . .

"Is there a check-cashing service nearby?" Norah asked.

"Yes, ma'am. Two blocks over. Federated. Just off the corner of Broadway."

116

12

NORAH SAT in Captain Felix's office, legs crossed, relaxed, reporting.

"The manager of the check-cashing service wasn't inclined to be cooperative, but I convinced him." She smiled jauntily. "Going through his records, I found that every one of them— Laifer, Waggoner, Brady, Hoysradt, and Zelinsky—had cashed their Social Security checks at Federated. That includes the latest victim, Grace Swann."

"Good work."

"Luck, Captain, it was luck. The doorman out-and-out told me that the old people in the building spent the third of every month down in the lobby waiting for the mailman. After that it was just a matter of following from one thing to the next."

"That's what detective work is all about." Felix slid down low in the chair, stretched out his long legs, and cupping his chin in the palm of the right hand, supported the right elbow in his left hand. "Somebody has figured himself one hell of an ugly way to get money." He grimaced. "You think you've seen and heard it all, then something like this comes along. . . ." He reached one hand to the intercom and flipped a switch. "I want everybody on duty with Sergeant Mulcahaney's unit in here. Plus . . . Baum, Link, Brennan . . . and Schmidt." He raised his eyebrows at Norah. "You're going to get your additional personnel."

As they filed in, each one took note of who else had been called and particularly of Norah. When they were all assembled, Felix began.

"It looks like we've got something very big and particularly ugly on our hands." He swiveled his chair around so that he

117

could look at the oversized wall calendar to the left of his desk and by so doing drew everyone's attention to it. For a moment he let them stare at the full-color photograph of a peak in the Rockies, snow covered but with the first green shoots of spring peeping through around the base. "On the third of this month, two days ago, a Mrs. Grace Swann, age seventy-three, in relatively good health, died in her bed—apparently by natural suffocation."

That drew their eyes from the melting snow to the big red numeral below.

"As you know, we've had a rash of deaths by suffocation lately," Felix continued. "In Doc Osterman's opinion the number has risen well above the norm. He suggested we take a look at the circumstances surrounding this latest one. Augie went to the scene."

Everybody eyed Baum.

"Don't worry about it, Augie," Felix reassured him. "I went over it myself. I knew something wasn't right, but I couldn't put my finger on it either. So I decided we needed somebody who understood the feminine mystique."

That meant Norah. They acknowledged that she was back on the case with a nod or a grin in her direction.

Felix continued. "It appears that on the afternoon of her death Mrs. Swann fixed herself a cup of tea. The setup was for one, but the way Norah reads the scene, Mrs. Swann was not alone. For one thing, she had brought out her best silver and her good china, and there was an extra, broken cup in the trash." Before Augie Baum could voice his objection, Felix parried it. "Plus at least half a dozen perfectly edible cookies. Now, the cup certainly might have been broken and thrown out by the victim herself, but nobody as short of money as Mrs. Swann would sweep half a dozen delicious butter cookies into the garbage. If she didn't want them, she'd return them carefully to the box or to a cookie jar.

"So it looks like her visitor could have been her killer. He could have grabbed her, covered her mouth and nose with a scarf or pillow, and when she was either unconscious or perhaps even dead, dragged her into the bedroom, knocking over the teacup in the process. He undressed her and put her

118

in her bed to make it look as though the suffocation had occurred naturally during sleep. He got rid of every sign of his presence by throwing out the broken cup and putting away the extra silverware. Maybe he didn't know where the cookies belonged or just couldn't be bothered to put them away and threw them out instead." Felix folded his hands on top of his blotter and looked around for comments or questions.

"What was the motive?" David Link asked.

"Robbery."

"Had the place been searched?"

"Not necessary. He knew the cash was in her purse and that it was all she had."

David scowled.

"It was the third of the month," Felix explained. "The day Social Security checks are delivered—and cashed."

"God!" David paled.

"As soon as Mrs. Swann received her check, she rushed out to cash it—like everybody else. Then she bought food and a few items at the drugstore. Deducting the amounts of the cash-register slips we found in her handbag from the amount she cashed at Federated, she figures to have had two hundred and sixty-four dollars in cash when she got home—plus whatever extra she had from before."

Brennan groaned.

"It could have been the kid who delivered the groceries," Schmidt suggested.

"She carried the groceries home herself," Norah told him. "Most old people do; for one thing, they don't often buy in large enough quantities to warrant delivery, and then they're afraid to let a stranger inside the apartment."

"Somebody at the market could have seen her flash her roll," Schmidt mused.

Baum didn't agree. "It could have been anybody. The muggers are out in force at the start of the month just looking for those green government checks."

"Why in God's name don't these people have the checks sent to the bank?" Brennan exclaimed, and his voice quavered. "Why do they think the law was formulated?"

For Brennan to show such emotion was an event in itself.

119

Felix placated him. "The law is new. A lot of them don't know about it yet."

"We're not talking about an ordinary mugger, Roy," David pointed out. "This guy didn't follow her to her building and upstairs to her apartment and then strong-arm his way in. She served him tea."

"So she knew him; so that makes it easier," Baum grunted. "Or ought to," he qualified glumly.

Felix said, "You know, every one of the known and suspected victims in the Westvue also cashed her checks at Federated."

Augie Baum let out a long, low whistle. David Link nodded as though he had been expecting just this. Brennan, in control once more, said nothing but his face was grim.

"That makes six," Gus Schmidt observed in awe.

"That we know of," David corrected.

His words hung in the silence of Captain Felix's office as acrid and palpable as cigarette smoke in still air. Felix was not surprised that Link should so quickly grasp the full implication. A quick glance at Norah told him that she had been ahead of David, ahead of all of them. And Brennan, usually measuring the height and breadth of an obstacle while the other two had already hurtled over it to the finish line, wasn't far behind on this one.

"Creep . . ." David muttered. "Cold-blooded creep."

"But smart," Felix said. "It's pretty hard to prove murder without a body, but he's left us the bodies and we still can't prove a thing. If Norah hadn't come up with the Federated Check-Cashing Service as the connection between the deaths, we wouldn't know where to look or have any reason for looking."

David winked at her, Brennan bestowed a solemn nod, and Schmidt an avuncular smile. Augie Baum moved one step closer to her; later, outside, he'd slap her on the back, make a big thing out of his support.

"So. As of now you're all working for the Senior Citizens Squad." He nodded to Norah.

She made the assignments. "Gus and Augie, here's the list of the women who've cashed Social Security checks at Federated during the past two years; check it against the ME's files of unattended deaths. Also CUPI's. If a name appears on both lists, get the date and cause of death, age of victim, health . . . and so forth."

"Right."

"Roy, a full history on Grace Swann. As far as we know now, she had no living relatives, but make sure. Then check her friends, her activities, where she shopped, who she talked to—the whole bit. I have a feeling that the killer is someone she knew casually, maybe somebody she talked to at the market or the newsstand or wherever. He's not going to be easy to pick out, but give it your best shot."

"Right, Sergeant."

"That leaves the employees at Federated. David and I will check them out."

"Wouldn't they be bonded?" David asked. "In which case the bonding company would have investigated them pretty thoroughly."

Felix picked that up. "You willing to run this case secondhand?"

"I was just trying to avoid a duplication of effort. Sorry, Captain."

"I don't think our man would have done anything a bonding company could pick him up on." Norah smoothed things over. "What we're dealing with—well, obviously he's not a beginner, not anymore; let's call him a talented amateur. I think we have to double-check everything and then check it once more after that."

Felix nodded and that was the dismissal. Everybody filed out. Nobody had said a word about how all this would affect Lieutenant Capretto's situation. Not even Norah. She'd hung back for a private word with the captain, then changed her mind. They'd already covered the subject. Besides, what she did or didn't do now, whether or not she was part of the investigation, no longer mattered. The case had got too big, gathered too much momentum.

The Federated Check-Cashing Service was a small operation with a manager, one secretary, and three clerks. None of

121

them was in debt. None lived beyond his means—though God only knew what wild extravagances a monthly Social Security allotment could provide, even as supplementary income. Neither the manager nor any of the employees had a sick mother, wife, or child who might require special medical treatment—in which case the allotment wouldn't go far either. In sum, none of the people at Federated appeared a likely suspect.

Gus and Augie had come up with two more apparently natural deaths that fitted the pattern and must now be considered suspect. Both had occurred within the same area as the ones under investigation—one in an apartment building on Broadway and Seventy-fifth, the other around the corner from the Museum of Natural History. That brought the count up to eight and meant that each of the five Federated employees had to be checked out against eight possible homicides. Every detective on the case had worked longer and more tedious odds.

It was always possible for one investigator to catch what another had overlooked, so Norah made sure that neither she nor David interviewed the same employees on the second round. Of course, it was unrealistic to expect hard alibis for each of the eight dates in question. Norah didn't expect it. Pick a date and ask someone what he was doing, where he was. Nobody remembered. Isolate one day from all the rest. It can't be done. Not unless something memorable happened. It could be a world-shaking thing—everyone recalls what he was doing when he heard the news of President Kennedy's assassination—or it could have purely personal significance, but there had to be a reason for remembering. What Norah was looking for was a means of eliminating as many of the Federated people as possible. Then they could move on, though she didn't know to what.

Two of the crimes had been committed during the first week of June and the first week of July. Vacation time. Any of the personnel out of the city either of those weeks would be automatically free of suspicion.

As it happened, the job was made easier by the fact that all the deaths occurred on weekdays, and subject to certain flexibility in estimating the exact time of death because of the lapse before some of the bodies were discovered, most of the deaths had occurred during the business day. It remained only to verify the attendance records of the employees. There were no unexplained absences on any of the pertinent dates.

"Washout." Looking disgusted, but far from discouraged, David dropped his report on Norah's desk, pulled up a chair, and sat down beside Roy Brennan for an impromptu conference.

"Doesn't have to be an employee," Brennan pointed out. "Could be one of the other clients. There's a line of them every month waiting to get their money. They probably get to talking, get on friendly terms. Later, when the doorbell rings and the intended victim answers and sees her buddy from the line . . . well, she's got no reason not to let him in."

"If we're going to check out each and every client on the line, then we've got to check every merchant in the area, every passerby. Pick something hard, will you, Roy?"

"It wouldn't be an old person," Norah reminded them. "The killer had to have plenty of physical strength."

David nodded, deep in thought. "How about a stakeout? We could stake out Federated."

Norah frowned. "Assuming our man shows up and we spot him and tail him and his victim, we've got to catch him in the act. But we haven't a clue where they're going, so how are we going to take the necessary precautions to protect the victim? Tough."

"But not impossible."

"And we have to wait nearly three weeks for the next month's checks to be delivered," Roy observed, then sighed. "He could even skip a month. We're going to have to canvass the neighborhood."

Norah shook her head. "If he lives in the area, and both the captain and I think he does, then we'd be tipping our hand."

The three were silent for a while.

"How about a former employee, somebody who used to work for Federated?" David offered. "Maybe he got fired, bears a grudge, and is ripping off the old folks for revenge."

Norah indicated the phone. "What've we got to lose?"

David dialed the number they all knew by heart.

"Mr. Borgen? This is Detective Link. Sorry to trouble you

again, sir. . . . Well, I wish I didn't have to take up your time, sir, believe me, but this will be brief. We are interested in former employees of the company. Could you give me the names of people who worked for you, let's say within the last two years, and either quit or were fired?"

As he listened, it occurred to David that for a man who said he had no time, Ernest Borgen was going into a lot of unnecessary detail. "What's his name?" David asked, and jotted it down on the pad Norah pushed toward him. "Is that so? He wanted to come back, but you wouldn't take him. When was that, do you remember? . . . Yes, well, when did he quit? . . . How about his last paycheck? You'd have a record, wouldn't you? . . . Yes, I'll hold."

David covered the mouthpiece. "They don't have much of a turnover, but there was one guy who quit sometime last year. He's looking up the exact date. The guy wanted—" He broke off. "Yes, Mr. Borgen, I'm still here. Way back then, eh? . . . No, no, that's very helpful. Thank you. I appreciate —" Again David had to listen to the manager's apologia. "I understand you couldn't rehire him. Certainly I understand. . . . No, no, I don't blame you one bit. If the man proved unreliable the first time, there would be no reason to suppose—" He wasn't allowed to finish. Grimacing, David held out the phone so that both Norah and Roy could hear the squawk of Borgen's protestations.

At the manager's first pause for breath David cut in firmly. "Thank you again. . . . No, sir, you can be assured that we will not reveal where we got the information."

He hung up. "Looks like we might have something. Fellow's name is Leon Eilbott and he lives right around the corner from Mrs. Swann, or at least he used to. He worked for Federated for about four months into the middle of January last year. Good worker, punctual, steady, reliable. Then suddenly, one day, without any kind of advance notice, he turned in his cashbox and quit. Just like that."

Norah raised her eyebrows. "Didn't give a reason?"

"Oh, yeah. Said he had something better. Got himself a part in a Broadway show. He's an actor."

"Actors will drop anything, the best and most secure job in

124

the world, for a bit part in a third-rate road company," Norah observed.

"Borgen knows it and that's why he's mad," David replied. "He claims that Eilbott gave him references from a bank on the West Coast where he'd worked, but he never mentioned he was an actor. If he had, Borgen wouldn't have hired him."

"Probably why Eilbott didn't mention it," Roy observed.

"This is where it gets interesting," David continued. "About six weeks after he quit, Eilbott turned up wanting his job back. Seems the show folded out of town. Borgen was indignant. Told Eilbott he couldn't just come and go as he pleased. He turned him down cold and also warned him not to give Federated as a reference because he, Borgen, was going to inform all parties that Eilbott was unreliable."

Norah consulted the timetable. "If this Eilbott quit in mid-January and turned up six weeks later, that would bring it just to the beginning of March—which is when the first victim at the Westvue, Phoebe Laifer, was strangled."

Roy shook his head. "I don't see this Eilbott running around killing old ladies to spite Borgen or ruin his business. If that were the motive, wouldn't he have left clues pointing to Borgen and Federated? Wouldn't he have proclaimed the injustice, sent letters to the newspapers, made phone calls, something? He not only made no attempt to call attention to Borgen, he covered up the very fact of murder."

"Right, right. He didn't do it to spite Borgen. He did it for the money. It's that simple. He did it for the money." David's face was carefully blank, his eyes steady, fixed on the far wall past the top of Norah's head. "If he could lay his hands on three hundred or so a month, he wouldn't need to scrounge around for temporary jobs to support himself while he waited for his agent to call. He wouldn't have to tie himself down as a clerk or salesman from nine to five; he could be out doing theatrical rounds, auditioning, taking classes . . . whatever. He's not greedy; he's not living high; he's satisfied just to get his rent and grocery money every month. He's a modest, reasonable man."

You couldn't bleed for every victim, they all realized, or you'd be bled dry in a week. A cop retreated into humor; a cop was quick with the gag as protection against the daily horrors of the job. But this one was beyond laughs, so David leaned heavily on the sarcasm. It didn't really help.

"He tried to make each allotment last as long as possible," David went on. "When he runs short, he just hangs around Federated for one of the old dolls to go in and get her money. He's choosy. He wants one who's real old and feeble and not likely to put up much resistance."

According to Roy, crimes of violence were deplorable, and further comment was neither necessary nor helpful. Emotions obscured the intellect, got in the way of impartial investigation. Emotions were for amateurs. "Even an old lady isn't going to stand still while she's being suffocated," he commented.

David continued with his reconstruction. "He follows the intended victim home. He has to be sure that she lives alone . . . so that means he has to know something about her. And she has to know him, of course, well enough to admit him. She might remember him from his days at Federated, but that was a long time ago. Maybe he's taken the trouble to strike up an acquaintance more recently. . . ."

"Maybe he's worked up some kind of ruse to get in," Roy suggested.

"He could say that he's from Federated . . . claim that the old lady got shortchanged—by accident, naturally. He's full of apologies. He offers the intended victim a five- or ten-dollar bill, but he needs a signed receipt. You can bet he gets invited inside!" David's voice quickened. He wasn't looking at the wall anymore. "Once inside it's easy. He overpowers her, undresses her, and puts her to bed with the pillow over her face. If she's a rummy, he doesn't even have to bother to take her clothes off. No weapon, no fingerprints, no indication that a murder was even committed. Neat, efficient, untraceable." Then he added, so low that Norah and Roy barely heard, "He's got to be some kind of monster."

"But Mrs. Swann was neither that old nor that feeble," Norah reminded him.

"So she struggled and that's how the teacup got broken. Or he slipped something into her tea—a minimal amount of

126

some tranquilizer, enough to lower her resistance but not enough to show up in the autopsy."

David was close, but . . . something was missing, and Norah didn't quite know what. She was surprised, though, that David should be assuming facts to support a theory. It was one of the very first pitfalls they had both been warned against—by Joe. She was even more surprised that she should be aware of it, whereas David was not. She decided not to say anything directly. "Between the two of you you've worked up a good, plausible case—on the basis of a single phone call to Ernest Borgen. Don't you think we have to find out something about this Eilbott before we apply for a warrant?"

Certainly it was most unlike Norah Mulcahaney, the emotional and impulsive one, to caution the other two.

"First we've got to check his employment record. We've got to know exactly when he was working and when he wasn't. If he quit Federated in January of last year to go into a Broadway show, then he has to be a member of Actors Equity. He could also belong to the Screen Actors Guild and AFTRA. One of the unions will be able to tell us whether or not he has an agent. Of course, we want to make sure that Eilbott doesn't know we're interested in him."

David sighed aggrievedly.

"I'm sorry if I'm underscoring the obvious, David."

"I get the impression you don't like my reconstruction."

"I'll like it better when we get some facts to support it." Surprising how rank changed one's point of view. "On the other hand, not only is Eilbott all we've got—he has the one single, indispensable qualification to be a suspect."

Roy was openly curious. David was somewhat wary, but he had to ask: "What?"

"As an actor Eilbott would be either unemployed or working at night. Since every one of the deaths occurred during the daytime, he's the only one we know who doesn't have an automatic alibi."

13

ON OCCASION actors do work in the daytime—they rehearse in the daytime; they do daytime television and radio; motion pictures are filmed in the daytime and so are commercials—but what Norah had really meant was that actors do not keep regular office hours, and to that extent Leon Eilbott did not have a built-in alibi. For Norah not only liked David's theory, she liked it so much she was afraid to commit herself to it without solid evidence. Getting information turned out to be easy. At Actors Equity David was handed the *Players Guide*, a compendium of just about every actor in New York. The actors on the West Coast had their own separate book. Each entry in the *Guide* consisted of name and telephone-service number—if the actor had a telephone service and usually he did since casting directors were notoriously impatient and given to calling someone else if the first choice wasn't around to answer his telephone. Also included were physical description, professional credits, agency and union affiliations. Ninety percent of the entries were accompanied by a photograph; the other ten percent represented Equity members who were so down on their luck that they couldn't afford the added cost of having the picture taken and published. Leon Eilbott was among the ninety percent who could.

He had a disarmingly pleasant face, Norah thought as she studied the photograph in the copy of the *Players Guide* that David placed in front of her. In Madison Avenue parlance, Eilbott had a *sincere* look. Dark blond, with a small, neat head and small, neat features. According to the description, he was five nine and a half, weighed 150. He was supposed to be thirty-five years old, but Norah thought he looked younger.

Possibly he was using an early photo. He was a member of both Actors Equity and the Screen Actors Guild, and he worked out of several theatrical agencies—exclusive representation evidently being reserved for the top stars.

It was then merely a matter of collating the union records and the casting-agency records to make up Eilbott's professional-employment profile for the past couple of years. Aside from the Broadway show for which he'd quit his job at Federated but which had never reached Broadway, the record was not impressive. He'd done a couple of TV commercials, appeared as a contestant on one TV game show, toured briefly in the fall with an industrial show—the kind of thing presented at conventions. He had been "at liberty" more often than working. Not that it was anything to be ashamed of. According to the statistics kept by the actors unions, Eilbott's situation was typical. Of the 12,000 members of Actors Equity, for example, 3,000 were employed, which meant that 9,000 were out of work—not an impressive average. It seemed to Norah that the glamour was superficial and that the chances of joining the select group that managed to eke out a living in their chosen profession was too much of a long shot on which to base one's life. But many did.

Next they examined Leon Eilbott's nonprofessional-employment record. According to the New York State Unemployment Service, the only nonacting job he'd held during the last sixteen months was the one at Federated. He had applied for benefits after Borgen refused to rehire him, but as he had not worked for the required number of weeks during the year, he was informed that he was not eligible. He had not reapplied. Either he'd found steady employment or he hadn't needed the money. A check of the employment records for Social Security deductions revealed he had not had any kind of employment.

Eilbott was not married. Discreet inquiries around his building indicated he had no steady girlfriend. He had plenty of visitors, male and female, but these were thought also to be actors who came to rehearse scenes for classes or auditions. In other words, Leon Eilbott was dedicated to one thing only—his career. Copies of the *Players Guide* picture were shown around, but none of the tenants of the Westvue or of any of the other buildings in which the victims or suspected victims had lived remembered having seen him.

"The point is that they would have had no reason to take particular notice of him." Norah was trying to justify the lack of evidence while reporting to Felix. She was surprised herself at how much she'd been counting on validating David's theory. "We haven't come up with a thing, not a single hard fact. We can't even prove murder was committed, much less pin it on Eilbott—or anybody else."

That, of course, was the heart of the problem, always had been. Felix waited, expecting Norah's natural optimism to reassert itself, but she just sat dejectedly.

"So we're back to the stakeout," he said. "At least we know who we're looking for."

"I wish we didn't have to sit around and wait for two weeks."

"You have a better idea?"

"We could put a tail on him."

"We know he's not going to act till a certain date." Norah was floundering, and they both knew it. "We agreed that the last thing we want is for Eilbott to have any inkling that we're suspicious. We have no choice but to wait till the third of May."

It wasn't only because the investigation was stalled that Norah was depressed, but because she was lonely. It had been exactly seventeen days since Joe had moved out, fifteen days since he'd called to let her know where he could be reached. She hadn't heard from him since.

The lectures were over, and she had nothing to do with herself. Before, she had been anxious to see and talk to her father, but he had avoided her; now he was the one calling and she the one making excuses. She was simply not in the mood for advice and afraid that sympathy would make her break down completely. Before, there had been the constant obligation of visiting Joe's mother. Actually, Norah had become very fond of Signora Emilia, but it was sometimes difficult to squeeze the visits into their schedule, but squeezed in they had to be. Now that there was plenty of time, she could hardly go alone. Or could she? Would Joe think she was trying to enlist his mother's aid in getting him back?

How was she going to get Joe back? So far she hadn't done a thing. What was she supposed to do that she hadn't already done? Or say that she hadn't already said? She'd admitted her fault, admitted that she shouldn't have gone behind his back. She had promised not to do it again. She would not beg him to come back. She wanted him—oh, God, yes! But he would have to want her, too.

Norah believed in meeting problems head-on. But not this time. To press might mean—not divorce, she wouldn't even let herself think of that and she didn't believe that Joe, as a good Catholic, would consider it, but annulment was not beyond possibility. Joe had said that they should have time. How much time? How long could they go on like this?

It was hard to fill the hours. Norah's house was as clean as it could be; there was just nothing more to scrub or polish or vacuum. She started on her wardrobe. There was mending to be done, and all the skirts she had put up a couple of years back needed to be let down again—hardly an engrossing occupation. Nevertheless, she got out the sewing basket, turned on the stereo, then turned it off again—the records had all been selected by Joe; she didn't want to hear them. Essentially a solitary person, she had never before felt lonely. Maybe she should get a pet? It wouldn't be fair to get a dog and then leave him home alone for most of the day. Cats didn't mind being alone. She could get a cat. There was only one thing wrong: She didn't like cats. What she wanted was Joe. She wanted Joe to come home. To just be there. Even if they weren't speaking, just to have him in the house . . . his presence. . . .

She was starting on the second skirt when the doorbell rang. Her heart stopped, then started again with a sharp stab of hope in her chest. She set the sewing aside, gave herself a quick inspection in the mirror, then opened the door.

"Oh. Hi, Dad."

She tried to hide her disappointment, then forgot about it in her surprise at his companion. "Hello, Mrs. Fitzgerald. How are you?"

"I'm fine. Thank you, Mrs. Capretto." The housekeeper's eyes were bright, her cheeks rosy with embarrassment.

"Aren't you going to let us in?" Mulcahaney asked.

"Oh. Sorry. Sorry, Dad. Of course." She stepped aside. What was going on here?

Her father's booming tone as he took a stand in the center of the living room indicated that he wasn't exactly at ease himself. "Sit down, Eileen." He indicated the sofa to Mrs. Fitzgerald. "Norah, you sit, too. I have something to say and I want you to sit and listen quietly. You'll be wondering why Eileen and I have dropped in on you like this. . . ." He took a breath. "The reason is twofold, the first part being the situation between you and Joe. If it weren't for that, we wouldn't be here, Eileen and me. We wouldn't have had the nerve to come. So I guess there's good in everything because you should know. You have a right to know."

"What are you talking about, Dad? Will you get to the point?"

"Well, will you sit down? Both of you. You make me nervous standing there, sizing each other up like a couple of prize-fighters."

"Dad!"

Mrs. Fitzgerald turned even rosier.

"I'm sorry. Eileen, sit down, please. Norah, have a little patience. What I have to say. . . . You remember how anxious I was to see you married? I always told you that the saddest thing is to be alone, not to have anybody that gives a damn whether you live or die, not to have anybody to come home to."

"I didn't turn Joe out. He was the one who wanted to leave."

"I know. He told me. He came up to the apartment and we talked. Now, I'm not taking sides—"

"He shouldn't have done that. I didn't go to his mother. . . ."

"All he said was that you'd had a disagreement; he didn't say about what. He thought you should both have a cooling-off period."

"I'm not going to say any more either."

"I didn't think you would."

That was another surprise, that her father wasn't going to try to pry it out of her and then press his good advice on her.

"Mind you," Mulcahaney continued, "I think sharing the

132

problem would relieve you. I never thought I'd live to say it, but—maybe you should go to a marriage counselor."

"Dad!" She'd never thought she'd live to hear it.

"You should unburden yourself, sweetheart. Personally, I think it would be a lot easier to tell your troubles to someone close, someone who cares—like me. Cheaper, too."

Norah had to smile; that was more like it.

"All right, all right. I'm not trying to force a confidence out of you. That's not why I'm here."

"Why are you here?"

"I'm trying to tell you if you'll give me a chance." He glared; Norah sighed; Mrs. Fitzgerald kept out of it. "You see, I figure the problem between you and Joe is that you don't talk to each other."

"Is that what you came to tell me?"

He went right on. "You talk, but you don't say anything. You don't say what's in your hearts. You're both at fault: you because you go ahead and make decisions on your own; Joe because he lets you get away with it."

"So you're on his side."

"I'm not on anybody's side. I told you, I'm not going to interfere."

"What do you call this?"

"I'm trying to explain why Eileen and I came over here. You see, I've been doing exactly what I'm blaming you and Joe for doing. I have no right to preach honesty if I'm not honest myself."

Norah was stunned. She waited and watched while, with a shyness that was distinctly new for Patrick Mulcahaney, he went over and sat down beside Mrs. Fitzgerald. He took her hand in his. "You thought Eileen was my housekeeper. She's not. She's . . . she's . . . we're in love."

Of all the various possibilities Norah had considered to account for her father's recent odd state she had never thought of this one simple answer. She was ashamed because she'd stopped thinking of him as an individual, relieved that he was all right, and sad because he'd been afraid to approach her sooner. Then she saw that he was watching her anxiously for approval.

133

She went over and kissed him on his withered cheek. "That's wonderful news, darling. Wonderful. I'm happy for you both." Her smile was as warm for Eileen Fitzgerald.

The look they shared, her father and Eileen, was one of quiet satisfaction. His hand gripped hers a little harder, and she squeezed back. There was no other overt sign of their feeling, yet it was an aura around them. They wore the new love they had found in their last years like a mantle and they wore it with dignity.

"Why didn't you say something that day I came over, Mrs. Fitzgerald? Why did you let me think you were the cleaning lady?" Norah asked.

"Her name's Eileen."

"I'm awfully sorry about that, Eileen."

"You were very complimentary about my work," Eileen Fitzgerald teased.

"You should have told me. You should have said something."

"I thought it should come from Pat. From your father."

"Dad." Norah was very gentle. "Why didn't you tell me? Why did you hold back?"

"I wasn't sure how you'd take it. I was afraid you might disapprove."

"Because of Mother? She's been gone such a long time. I'm glad you've found someone you care for and who cares for you and that you're not going to be alone anymore. When is the wedding?"

Hastily, Eileen Fitzgerald pulled her hand back from Mulcahaney's grasp and flushed violently. Her father was also distinctly embarrassed.

"You don't understand." Mulcahaney's gaze wandered around the room; he looked everywhere but at his daughter. "Eileen and I . . . we're. . . . She's moved in with me."

"You mean the day I came to see you she'd already. . . ."

Mulcahaney nodded.

"But you're not married?"

Her father shook his head.

Norah was shocked. This was not the time to analyze the depths of her disapproval and she tried hard to control it. She looked from one to the other. "It's not my place to criticize;

134

you're both adults and you know what you're doing, but I . . . I just don't understand. Why didn't you go to St. Joseph's and have the priest perform a short ceremony?"

"We're not going to get married."

That left her speechless.

Mulcahaney sighed. This time when he reached for Eileen Fitzgerald's hand it was a statement of intention. She let him take it and hold it tenderly and protectively. Now that the worst was out, words came more easily. "We want to get married. There's nothing in this world we want more, but we can't afford it. It's the Social Security law. As a widow Eileen gets full benefits each month. If she remarries, she relinquishes—"

"But she'll get benefits based on your earnings," Norah protested.

"Half. She'll get half."

"Oh, Dad . . . does it make that much difference?"

"I'm afraid it does. We've discussed it and we've decided that the way the economy is going we can't afford to get married. We'd be able to scrimp along now on the reduced income, but later on. . . . The apartment is rent-controlled, but there's no guarantee it always will be. Eileen's a thrifty shopper, but prices keep going up. Even now there's mighty little left for clothes or entertainment."

There was nothing new about the situation. A lot of elderly people seeking companionship and finding affection, even love, were forced by economics to "live in sin." Certainly Norah was aware of it. It was depicted on TV with accompanying smirks and snickers. But this was not situation comedy; this was real and it was happening to her father. As far as Norah was concerned, it didn't rate even an indulgent chuckle. Looking at her father's face, she could have wept for the humiliation she saw there.

Patrick Mulcahaney's background, standards, and religious beliefs were opposed to this illicit relationship. As for Eileen Fitzgerald, it was obvious that her background was similar, that she was devoted to Mulcahaney, but that her conscience bothered her and that her joy was tinged with guilt. There were Catholics who still believed in mortal sin and who feared excommunication.

135

Norah seethed. It wasn't fair. Her father and Eileen were entitled to self-respect and to respect from their peers. They should be able to proclaim their love, not forced to hide it. Eileen Fitzgerald shouldn't have to pose as the cleaning woman when she answered the door. A hot wave of shame for them all surged through Norah. Her father should be able to give Eileen his name.

"Joe and I would be glad to help you out." For a moment she forgot her own uncertain situation.

So did her father. "When the babies come, it may not be convenient. Besides, we want to be self-sufficient. We're not happy about the way things are, but. . . ." He shrugged.

"Have you talked to the priest?"

Mulcahaney shook his head. "If we persist in the sin, how can he offer us absolution?"

Joe was adjusting to his new life-style and not having any easier time of it than Norah. He was putting in a lot of hours at work, but inevitably he had to return to his hotel room. Inevitably he had time to think. What exactly did he expect to gain from this separation? He asked himself that over and over. Norah had already admitted that she had lacked trust, that she took too much on herself. She had promised to do better. What more did he want? What more could he expect? Some kind of guarantee? Then what? What was keeping him away from his wife when he was miserable and lost and unfulfilled without her?

As the weeks passed, Joe even began to question whether he was himself completely blameless. Had he overreacted? Had he moved out to give each one of them an opportunity for reassessment? Or was he subconsciously punishing Norah?

That was an ugly thought, and Joe brooded a long time before he rejected it. The fact remained that he had done very little honest self-appraisal during the separation period. He did spend a lot of time thinking about Norah, though, wondering what she was up to, how she filled her time, whether she was as lonely as he. He yearned to talk to her, to hear her voice. He could call. Why not? They'd set no ground rules that said he couldn't call. Perched on the edge of the bed in his hotel room, Joe stared at the telephone. How would Norah

136

feel about his calling? When she heard his voice, wouldn't she expect that he had worked things out? But things were no different now from what they'd been the night he walked out. So instead of calling Norah, Joe tried a couple of old phone numbers.

Two of the girls had moved away, and the numbers now belonged to strangers. Another was married and it was her husband who answered. Another wasn't at home. Celeste Keach was thrilled to hear from Joe after all these years.

"Long time no see," she murmured coyly.

"Well, I've been busy. Actually. . . ." What the hell, might as well give it to her straight. "I got married."

"Oh?" Some of Celeste's girlish pleasure abated.

"But we're not together right now."

"Oh? That's too bad." Celeste didn't mean it.

He took her to dinner at a restaurant she'd suggested and to which he'd never been. Nothing was right—the atmosphere, the service, the prices. God! The prices! His date's chatter grated on his nerves. All she did was talk about herself and clothes. He did recall that he'd never thought much of Celeste's brains, but she wasn't that gorgeous either. Had he ever thought she was? Finally Joe just tuned her out. After dinner he made the expected moves—she would have been insulted if he hadn't. He anticipated being turned down and had no intention of pressing, but she accepted. He had no choice but to bring her up to the room.

As they walked along the hotel corridor, Joe noticed a line of light under his door. He was sure he'd turned the light out before leaving, and it wasn't the kind of hotel where the maid came in to turn down the bed at night.

"Hold it," Joe whispered. With one hand he held Celeste back while with the other he drew his gun. Then he edged forward along the wall to his room, listening intently. There was no sound, no sound of any kind. Could Norah be in there? His heart started to pound. Could Norah have come, got the clerk to let her in? No. No, she wouldn't do that. If she did, she'd have the radio or television on. He grasped the doorknob firmly, turned it, and flung the door open, at the same moment lunging forward to cover the intruder with his gun.

A woman screamed.

137

"Mamma!"

Dressed in her Sunday black, relieved only by an heirloom lace collar and a small white-gold cross on a white-gold chain, Signora Capretto sat upright in the room's only chair.

"Mamma," Joe repeated.

"Oh, Dio mio, che scossa!" she clasped her hands over her heart. *"Come mi hai spaventato."*

Joe got down on his knees beside her. "I didn't mean to frighten you, Mamma. Are you all right?"

"Put that gun away. Put it away, *per l'amor di Dio.*"

"Sorry, Mamma, sorry. I saw the light under the door. I had no idea who was in here."

"Ah . . . ah. . . ." Her chest heaved up and down.

Now that he had got over his concern, Joe was annoyed. "Now, Mamma, there's nothing wrong with your heart. We both got a fright, okay? What are you doing here?"

"I came to see you, *figlio mio.* What else?"

"I know that. Why?"

"You would not come to see me." She shrugged, shoulders high and hands out in the elaborate Latin manner. Then her eyes strayed from Joe and fixed on a point over his shoulder. "I wished to talk to you about your *wife.*"

It needed neither her overly loud tone nor the deliberate underscoring of the crucial word for Joe to know that Celeste Keach had appeared in the doorway. Suppressing a sigh, he got up and turned around. "Mamma, this is Celeste. Celeste, my mother."

The two women looked at each other, and neither liked what she saw.

"It seems I have chosen an inconvenient time," Signora Emilia said with great formality, and rose.

"You should have let me know, Mamma."

"*Ah, si.* I will make an appointment."

"Mamma."

"So I'll be going." She smoothed the folds of her skirt and adjusted her handbag precisely over one arm.

Joe cast a look of helplessness at Celeste.

"I gotta be going myself, Joe," Celeste obliged. The mood couldn't be restored; the evening was shot anyway. "It's getting kinda late."

138

"It is at that," he agreed gratefully. It was ten o'clock. He looked from one to the other. He cleared his throat. "My mother lives in Brooklyn so I'll drop you off first, okay, Celeste?"

"Don't bother about me," his mother said. "I can take the subway."

"Don't bother about me," Celeste Keach assured him. "I can take a cab."

"Mamma, I am not going to let you ride the subway alone."

"That's how I got here."

He turned to his date. "If you're sure you don't mind taking a cab. . . ?"

"I don't mind."

She did mind, of course she did, and they both knew it. What could he do about it? He wanted to give her cab fare, but in front of his mother . . . it wouldn't look right. "You're sure?" he repeated helplessly.

"Yeah, I'm sure."

Still she waited. Of course she wanted the cab fare. He didn't blame her. Then Joe had an inspiration. "I'll go down with you and help you find a cab." He could give her the money then.

"Don't bother." Celeste Keach tossed her head.

The inspiration had come too late. "No, listen. . . ."

"Stay with your mamma." The blonde stalked to the door.

"I'll call you," Joe murmured under his breath as he saw her out. It was reflex. He didn't mean it, and she didn't hear it. If she had, Celeste Keach would wait for his call only for the pleasure of slamming the receiver down on him. He turned to his mother. Her face was stern, lips primly pursed, but there was no doubt that she had derived intense satisfaction from every moment of the exchange. Suddenly Joe grinned.

"It is not funny," Signora Capretto chided.

"Sure it is. Come on, Mamma, you know it is."

"No." She remained grim.

"Okay, Mamma. So now you're here you might as well sit down and say what you came to say."

"I see that it is no use. I am wasting my time."

139

"Okay, Mamma, if that's the way you want it. I'll drive you home."

"Are you going to get a divorce?" she asked abruptly.

Joe was stunned. "Of course not."

"An annulment?"

"No. We have no grounds. . . ."

"Then why aren't you living with your wife?"

"We've had a misunderstanding. I told you."

"Ah! A misunderstanding. I see. It must be very serious."

"Certainly."

"I will not ask what it is. If your wife has been unfaithful. . . ."

"No. Nothing like that."

"Or denied you your conjugal rights? Then, of course, you are fully justified in leaving her."

Joe flushed. These were not matters to be discussed with one's mother. "Mamma, don't involve yourself."

"She has not committed either of these sins?"

"Of course not."

Signora Emilia sighed heavily. "Something else, then? Well, what are you doing about it? Have you discussed this 'misunderstanding' with your wife?"

"She doesn't talk to me, Mamma. That's the problem."

"Ah? And the solution is for you not to talk to her. I see." She paused as though she were considering. "Well, are you seeking help? Have you consulted the priest perhaps?"

"You know I haven't."

"Then what are you doing, *figlio mio*? Waiting for the good God to perform a miracle on your behalf? I think he is waiting for you to help yourself."

14

NORAH MADE meticulous preparations for the stakeout. May 3 was a Saturday, so she checked the Planetarium Station of the post office to make sure there would be a local delivery. On the Friday, just before lunch, David Link stopped at her desk.

"I think we can forget about tomorrow."

"What?" She was startled. She had been thinking about Joe; she'd got into the habit of doing that more and more lately. "What do you mean?"

"I just had a call from Superior Artists, one of the agencies that handles Leon Eilbott. They just got him a job, an acting job. He's got a part in a movie for TV that's shooting in town. He starts tomorrow."

"No!"

"I'm afraid so."

"Damn."

"What's more, it's a good part, a feature role, his agent, Sol Weiss, tells me. They'll be on location here in New York shooting outdoors for at least a week, depending on the weather naturally. After that Eilbott will be moving on to Hollywood for the interior sequences. Looks like this is the break he's been waiting for. I don't think he's going to be ripping off anybody's Social Security money for a while."

Norah groaned.

"So?"

"We call it off? What else?"

They looked glumly at each other.

They had nothing on Leon Eilbott. They had no other suspect. They hadn't even proved the fact of murder. Neither

141

Asa Osterman's nor Norah's inferences—the one based principally on statistics, the other on personal interpretation of the scene of Mrs. Swann's death—were conclusive. She had been counting on the stakeout. She had been absolutely convinced that Leon Eilbott would show in the vicinity of the Federated office and that he would follow one of the old ladies who cashed a check. Difficult as the logistics were of covering a building without knowing in advance what building it would be, Norah had been certain that they could both have protected the intended victim and caught the killer in the act.

Captain Felix took the news in stride. He counseled patience, but in Norah's mind the case and Joe were still linked. Subconsciously she believed that solving the case would somehow result in a solution to their problems. She had no idea how it would come about—she wasn't even aware of thinking that it would—she only knew that having to call off the stakeout was a bitter setback.

"Any other ideas?" Felix asked.

"No, sir, not one in the world."

"Then we just have to wait."

"For what? Suppose he makes a big hit in this picture. Suppose he never needs to steal another dollar. Does that mean he gets away with it?"

"If it is Eilbott, if we read him right and he was doing it only for the money . . . then yes."

Norah couldn't accept that. Every instinct rebelled at the thought that he might never be brought to account for eight murders. It was galling, it was frustrating that there was nothing to be done, no clues to be chased down, no witnesses to be interrogated. Somewhere, sometime, Eilbott must have made a mistake, one mistake at one of the scenes. He must have left one clue: dropped a book of matches, caught a sleeve on a nail, been scratched perhaps and dripped one drop of blood. Or maybe he carried something away with him unknowingly: dust in his trouser cuff, a stain of some sort—fresh paint, special furniture polish. . . .

Something must have happened during the commission of one crime that would trip him up. Something unexpected, an accident, a contingency for which he had not made provision.

142

Otherwise Leon Eilbott had committed not only the perfect crime but a string of them. Norah wouldn't accept that either. There were no perfect crimes. None. Ever. Oh, crimes did remain unsolved, certainly, but that was because the investigator gave up.

She sat up most of the night reviewing the reports on the eight victims. She didn't discover anything new in the files, but she did get the glimmer of an idea. During the night it grew, and when she awoke the following morning, she knew what she would do. Actually, Norah thought with a tingle of excitement that she hadn't experienced in a long time, what she had in mind was just a ruse, even less—a gimmick to approach Leon Eilbott and talk to him without arousing his suspicion.

She had thought she might have to put on her uniform, but a quick check with the agency involved revealed that she did not. The occasion called for a skirt, however; she should look as feminine and pretty as possible. When she was ready, Norah surveyed herself critically and liked what she saw. She looked jaunty and carefree, and that was how she felt.

April had been much like March, raw, unseasonably cold, the winds often gusting close to gale force. But today was one of the rare days—bright sunshine and dry, clear air apparently distilled of impurities as though the city were under a giant dome and a vacuum had sucked out the foulness. Maybe such days seemed better than they actually were because they came so seldom; certainly they made the city seem not merely livable but a good place to be. The arrival of spring was even more evident inside Central Park. Norah was instantly struck by the sweep of purple blossoms of the rhododendron around the children's playround. Farther ahead, scrawny forsythia flanking the underpass had been transformed into graceful sprays of gold that swayed gently as mobiles in the breeze. She inhaled, squared her shoulders, thrust out her chin, and strode ahead. Unfortunately inside the tunnel it was still damp and the usual stench of garbage and urine persisted, but that didn't affect Norah's spirits. She hurried through.

A slight rise brought her up to the Mall and from there she could look toward Sheep Meadow, where the shooting was taking place.

The whole thing was on a much smaller scale than she had

143

expected. She saw only one camera, but this was mounted at the top of a crane, which in turn was mounted on a mechanized platform, a dolly. The people seated below were obviously the director and his assistant. There weren't as many spectators as she'd expected either. If they'd been shooting out on the street, a crowd would have gathered in minutes; there would have been barricades and police. But few came to the park this early. Not that it mattered. Norah wasn't trying to hide her presence. She joined the small group of spectators just as the action began.

The dolly moved forward cumbersomely, the camera rolled, two actors on bicycles entered the scene—a man and a girl.

The man was Eilbott. He was perhaps a few years older than he appeared in the picture in the *Players Guide*, possibly in his late thirties, but Norah recognized him right away. Neither the photograph showing his small neat head and neat features nor the description—dark blond hair, brown eyes—could convey the quality he exuded. To term it magnetism would be too general, but there was something . . . elusive and at the same time tangible. Norah stole a look at the people around her and noted that they were all watching Eilbott rather than the girl—and she was a pretty girl. The way he leaned toward her, the smile he gave her—a smile that reached up and into his eyes. He looked at her as though they were the only people in the world, as though he cared only for her. Maybe the intensity of his concentration was the secret; at any rate, he made the audience feel privileged intruders, each one holding his breath so as not to give away his presence. Norah couldn't hear the dialogue, but actors in movies didn't project the way they did on the stage, and that added to the sense of privacy and caused Norah, as it did everyone else, to strain forward and compensate by watching even more avidly. It was hard to envision this engaging man committing murder, killing eight old women in a manner that was both sly and ruthless.

She reminded herself that he was an actor and that she was watching him at his trade. Then the director yelled "cut." There was a *sotto voce* consultation with the technicians, then the director went into a huddle with his actors. The audience

144

came out of its collective trance. After a few moments the actors returned to their original positions; the whole thing started again.

This time Norah watched the girl, and it seemed to her that she was giving a better account of herself—that she was more believable, but that it wasn't through her own skill but rather a response drawn from her by Eilbott, a response to Eilbott's compelling sincerity. If he had appeared at the door, not one of those forlorn old ladies could have denied him entrance.

When the movie scene was repeated for the third time, Norah stopped watching. There was no doubt that Eilbott could have gained admittance, that he had the strength to overcome the frail victims. Did he have an alibi for any one of the pertinent times? He'd be leaving for Hollywood soon, and closer inquiries could be made in his absence.

"Cut! Take ten."

The announcement jolted Norah out of her reverie. She saw that the director was huddling with his crew and that Eilbott and the young actress were heading in the direction of the trailer. Norah ran after them.

"Excuse me, Mr. Eilbott?"

He turned. "Yes?"

"I'm sorry to bother you, but I'm from the mayor's Office for Film Making. I wonder if you could spare me a couple of minutes?"

"Oh? You bet. Sure."

The actress hesitated and, seeing that she was not included, withdrew. Eilbott waited till she was gone, then bestowed an engagingly diffident smile on Norah. "What can I do for you?"

"As you know, the mayor is very anxious to promote film production in New York. It's our responsibility not only to facilitate a legitimate movie company in getting the various necessary permits to shoot in the city, but also to cooperate in every way we can. So I'm down here to make sure that you have everything you need, give you any assistance . . ."

"That's certainly very nice, but—"

". . . Make sure that you have enough police to handle the crowds. . . ." It was only too obvious that there weren't any crowds and that the patrolman on duty wasn't paying

145

any attention to the few spectators that were there. Norah hurried on. "The mayor is very anxious that you should be courteously treated."

"I have been, absolutely, but I'm afraid, Miss . . . uh . . . ?"

She smiled up at him. "Norah. You can call me Norah."

"Well, Norah, everything's just fine, but I'm afraid you're talking to the wrong person. I don't have anything to do with the production."

"Oh, I know that. I already spoke to your production manager and to your director, Mr. Stanislas. . . ."

"Sadler," Eilbott corrected. "Stanislas is his first name."

"Really? Anyway, I thought that I should talk to the star, too."

He hesitated. "I'm not really the star."

"Ah, come on, Mr. Eilbott. Give me a break. Just a couple of questions?" She took out notebook and pencil.

"How can I refuse a pretty woman like you? Come on, let's find a place to sit down." He led her to a bench out of the way of both the movie people and the spectators. "Now, shoot."

"You've already indicated that you've been courteously treated by the police and by park personnel?"

"Absolutely."

"Do you have any suggestions for improving procedures for movie making in New York City?"

He shook his head. "I think it's all wonderful." His eyes were fixed on her face. "You know, you make quite a picture. The way the sun draws the gold flashes out of your hair, the blue sky, and that magnolia tree as backdrop—the camera should be on you."

The compliment, coming from a suspect, was unsettling. "Thank you."

"I haven't seen a woman blush like that since . . . since grade school. Oh, please, I'm not making fun of you. It's charming."

What was happening here? Was it possible that Leon Eilbott was baiting her? The possibilities tumbled through Norah's mind. Could he have seen her picture in the paper in connection with the Senior Citizens Squad? Had he recognized her?

"Could I ask you something personal?" she countered.

"Just about anything."

146

He could be acting, but the way he said it was reassuring.
"Doesn't it get boring having to do the same little bit of action
over and over and over again?"
"After a while, sure. It's up to the actor to find nuances to
sustain his own interest."
"Is it always like this? I mean, it doesn't seem very
glamorous."
The actor laughed. "The glamor is highly overrated, I'll
grant you. It's a rough business. There just isn't enough work,
and too many people who don't belong trying to get what
work there is and making it harder for those who are qualified. But it has its rewards. And I don't mean money necessarily. I'm talking about the opportunity for self-expression.
The stage is the most satisfying of all, though it's repetitious,
too, but in a different way."
"You've been on the stage?" Norah made herself sound
naïve and very impressed. "On Broadway?"
"Not exactly. I was in a Broadway show, but it closed out of
town."
She knew that, of course. She knew the date of the opening
and the closing and how much Leon Eilbott had been paid.
"What happens in a case like that?"
He shrugged. "You go out and look for another job."
"Okay, people, let's go. Places, please. Places."
The actor cast a quick look over his shoulder, noting that
the crew was ready and the actress with whom he played the
scene already straddling her bike. "Listen, Norah, you going
to be around for a while? I'll buy you lunch."
"Well. . . ." She hesitated: There weren't that many more
questions she could ask without arousing suspicion. "Thanks,
but I have to get back to the office."
"Dinner, then. Come on, how about dinner tonight?"
She shook her head. "I don't think so."
"Listen, no strings. Honest." He held out his hands, palms
up. "Look, no hands—that's a promise. Just dinner. What do
you say?"
"Come on, people. Let's go." The production manager was
getting annoyed. "How about it, Leon?"
"Coming, coming. Norah—I'll pick you up at seven. Where
do you live?"

147

"Uh . . . no. I'll meet you." Then she remembered to ask, "What's your address?"

His eyes widened, but he recovered quickly, found a card in his wallet, and scribbled on the back. As he handed it to her, he asked, "You're not planning to stand me up, are you?"

"Eilbott! You're on!"

"How'm I doing?" Even as he made the traditional response, the actor winked at Norah and ran for his position.

Norah watched the scene start, then slowly walked away.

Could she have made a mistake about Eilbott? Could they be focusing on the wrong man? Norah asked herself those questions a dozen times during the day. She could see Eilbott committing murder in an explosion of rage and passion. The man she had met this morning wasn't the type to choose an old lady at random, follow her home, force his way into her apartment, and suffocate her whenever he ran short of the rent. Norah bit her lip. How could she make such a judgment on the basis of one brief meeting? Could she dismiss the possibility that he had identified her as a police officer and the whole thing was an act? Either way, act or not, the date was a tremendous opportunity.

She couldn't afford not to keep it.

For one thing, she'd be getting a look at Eilbott's place. Not that Norah expected to find any grisly mementos lying around. Assuming that he kept and displayed any ghoulish souvenirs, they would not be recognizable as such and not admissible as evidence unless discovered during a legal search backed up by a warrant. Certainly keeping the date would give Norah the opportunity to know Eilbott better, to observe him, and to discover his flaw.

So, then, why was she reluctant?

Physical fear didn't enter into it. She was no frail little old lady. She carried one gun in her shoulder-strap handbag and a second small backup weapon in a leg holster strapped to the inside of her left calf. Over the years she had become a good shot; if attacked, she could defend herself. No, that wasn't what she was nervous about. It was four years since Norah Mulcahaney Capretto had had a date with anybody but Joe. She was shy.

148

She rang Eilbott's bell at five after seven that evening. The door was opened almost immediately.

He gave her an intimate, disarming smile, flashing white, impeccably capped teeth. "I really didn't expect you to show."

"Why not?"

"I don't know. I just didn't. I'm glad I was wrong, though. Come on in."

Once over the threshold, Norah's professional curiosity came to the fore. Eilbott's place was half a block down from Central Park West in a remodeled brownstone. Certainly from the outside it couldn't compare to the Gothic splendors on the avenue, but inside it had style, and the style hadn't come cheap. The long, narrow, high-ceilinged room had been stripped of all architectural folderols except for a small mid-Victorian mantel, the walls painted white, the front bay window left uncurtained. The furniture was sparse—sofa, Eames chair (or a very good copy) and ottoman, butcher block and chrome coffee table. She needn't have worried about the significance of knickknacks: There weren't any, just a pair of oversized crystal ashtrays. A single geometric black-and-red print, which to Norah's untrained eye looked like a giant crossword puzzle, hung on one wall. On the opposite wall, however, there was a gallery of photographs, mostly eight-by-ten professional glossies, identically framed. It took only one glance to know that these represented Eilbott's professional life. She couldn't wait to get a closer look.

"Well?"

"Oh . . . I like it."

"Thank you, but what I meant was may I have your coat?"

"Oh, yes. Thank you." She let him help her off with it and watched as he carried it into the next room.

"How about a drink?"

"Scotch and water, please."

She started toward the sofa, settling for the Eames chair instead—she didn't want the situation to get too cozy. But when he came back from the kitchenette with the drink in his hand, he ensconced himself on the ottoman, pulling it close to her knees with a smile that was just a little mocking.

"Mind if I ask you a personal question?" Norah asked.

149

"I told you this morning—anything. Shoot."

"From what you said, the acting business is pretty uncertain. This is a very nice apartment, in a good neighborhood. You have the time and money for sports. . . ." She had noticed that some of the photographs depicted Eilbott on ski slopes and tennis courts.

He grinned. "You want to know if you can order steak tonight?"

Norah flushed, part of the embarrassment genuine. "I've never dated an actor before."

"Listen, I understand." He chuckled. "I'm a working actor, so you can order filet mignon if you like. And when I'm not working, my family helps me out. Okay?"

She lowered her eyes and sipped her drink. He had no family. Both parents were dead, and the paternal grandparents lived in Florida on meager income. That had been checked out along with everything else about Leon Eilbott. The lie was the first positive indication that the actor was not what he appeared to be. It made Norah feel less guilty about the deception, bolstered her confidence. Subtly the situation had shifted.

Eilbott went on. "They're not rich, you understand, but they've got a little of the green stashed away. A lot of parents don't approve of show business. They think acting is . . . well, not manly, for one thing, and for another, they don't consider it real work. But my folks aren't like that. They believe in me. They're glad to help me out."

Why the elaboration of the lie? Why the almost compulsive justification?

"It's nice that you don't have to take all sorts of odd jobs to keep going like most actors."

"I'm lucky."

This time his smile was forced. Norah waited, but when he said no more, she asked, "Have you been in show business a long time?"

"Too long, considering the results—or lack of them. That's enough about me. Let's talk about you for a while."

"I'm nobody. Tell me some more about the picture. You won't have any trouble getting work after this, will you? You'll be famous."

"I'm afraid it takes more than one television movie to make

150

you famous, but"—he ducked his head modestly—"I do have a good part, a hell of a good part, and I think I'm good in it. It could be the break I've been waiting for." He sighed and stretched luxuriantly. "I was just about to give up when the call came. Ironic, isn't it? I'd just about decided it was hopeless. Oh, it's not that I haven't worked and had good parts, too. . . ." He gestured expansively to the rows of photographs. "But it was all small time—summer stock, off-off Broadway, even showcase. Nobody saw me, nobody that could do me any good—no agents, producers, like that. They tell you they have to see your work, so you take any job for peanuts, even for free. You rehearse a month and the show lasts a week. Then when you go to their offices, they say, 'Oh, sorry, we missed that one. Be sure to let us know next time.' Your notices don't mean anything; they're just so many pieces of paper."

"It sounds very hard."

"Demeaning. You have to lick everybody's . . . boots. From the receptionist to the producer. What really used to get my goat, still does, is the Trilbys."

"The what?"

"That's what I call the puppets, the performers that have no talent, that some *commedia dell'arte* director picks up off the street because they happen to look like his idea of the part. Then he has to teach them every inflection, every gesture."

"They don't last, do they?"

"They make it. They make it big." For a moment the raw need showed, glittering out of his eyes, ravaging his pleasant face like a consuming and crippling fever. Then it was gone. "How about you, Norah? Why don't you tell me a little about yourself? Don't you think it's about time?"

"There isn't much to tell."

"Sure there is. I sense all kinds of hidden depths."

"In me? No."

"How about your name? You realize you haven't even told me your full name?"

"What's in a name?"

"Could be a lot. An attractive young woman agrees to have dinner with me, to come to my apartment, but she won't tell me her name or where she lives. What am I expected to conclude from that?"

151

"I don't know." Norah was tense again.

"Obviously that she's married."

She relaxed. "We're separated."

Eilbott nodded. "I didn't think you were the type to play around. It still doesn't explain why you didn't want me to call for you."

"I'd rather not talk about it."

"Come on, Norah, something's bugging you. I can tell. You seem at ease and enjoying yourself, then all of a sudden you tighten up. Why don't you get it off your chest?"

She turned aside. He was too observant—fortunately he was making the wrong inferences.

"You're not afraid of your husband, are you?"

"That's silly." She could laugh at that.

"Because if you are . . . if he's hanging around bothering you. . . ."

"No."

"Is that why you didn't want me to come around to your place? Are you afraid that if he sees you going out with another man he'll make trouble? That's it, isn't it?"

"No, honestly."

"Have you called the police? You should."

Accident or calculation, that was too much. "Do you mind if we change the subject?" Norah got up and strolled over to examine the display of photographs. "Are these scenes from the plays and movies you've been in?"

"Plays and TV, yes."

"You certainly have a wide range."

"I used to be what the casting people call a 'character juvenile.' Now I'm too old to be a juvenile," he quipped.

"Do you do your own makeup? It's terrific. I can hardly recognize you in . . . some of these." Norah moved on. Finishing her drink quickly, she held out her glass. "Refill?"

Eilbott raised an eyebrow at the abruptness of the request but took her glass. "Coming right up."

As soon as he was gone, Norah returned to the photograph that had caught her attention. In it Leon Eilbott was dressed in a nineteenth-century frock coat and tall beaver hat. His hair was silvered and the hairline built down to a center peak on his

152

forehead, and he had a thin, elegant mustache so that his face appeared quite differently shaped. But it was the background which had caught Norah's attention—an outline of towers and crenellations which were generally accepted as representing Scotland in the same manner the Eiffel Tower symbolized France. In the lower right-hand corner was the play's title: *The Grave Robbers*.

As though from a distance, barely distinguishable through the roaring in her ears, she heard Eilbott call.

"Norah. . . ."

She jumped, thinking him at her shoulder, but he was still in the kitchen. She called back. "I'm sorry. What did you say?"

He stuck his head out. "You're wandering again. I asked what kind of food you were in the mood for tonight."

Her mind was racing. If one saw a picture of a young woman in an old-fashioned dress holding a bloody ax, the name immediately leaping to mind would be Lizzie Borden. So the title of the play, the background, and the actor's costume suggested to Norah a case famous in criminal annals. The parallel between that case and the murders she was presently investigating was inescapable. It had literally stunned her. The first thing she managed to do was move away from the photograph, then somehow she replied.

"What kind of food? Oh, I don't know. I leave it to you."

The photograph was not proof. Strongly presumptive, yes. As corroboration or what the art world calls provenance, intensely valuable, but there had to be more. What she needed was one piece of evidence, just one, to connect Leon Eilbott directly with any one of the eight victims.

She hadn't heard him come up behind her, didn't know he was there till she felt his warm breath on the back of her neck. He stood very close. His left arm encircled her waist. She tensed, holding her breath.

"Hey, you're real jumpy, aren't you?" he whispered, his mouth lightly brushing her hair. Then he brought his right arm around and put the drink in her hand.

Slowly Norah let her breath out again. Now she knew. She knew exactly how it had been done, how all those women, after the first two, had been killed without showing a mark.

153

What was more important, she had an idea how it might be proved. It was a long shot, but she had no doubt that it would pay off. The evidence was here, in this apartment, and tomorrow she intended coming back to find it, legally. She took the drink and, willing her muscles to relax, willing away the tension, turned—still within reach of Leon Eilbott's embrace.

"Thanks."

His eyes caressed her. "I was thinking . . . if you're nervous about being seen, maybe it would be a good idea to eat in? I'll just run over to the market, there's one open all night, pick up a couple of steaks. . . ."

"No, I'd rather not."

"You're the boss." He shrugged, his eyes releasing her. "It was just an idea."

"Some other time." Now it was safe to edge past him, but the thought of spending the rest of the evening with Eilbott, even in a public place . . . well, she didn't think she could maintain the pretense. Not now that she was sure of what he'd done. "If you don't mind, I think I should go home."

"You mean right now? Skip dinner?"

"I'm sorry."

Now she was determined to get away, and as Eilbott himself had provided a reason for her nervousness, she used it. "You were right, I'm more nervous about my husband than I realized. I'm sorry to spoil your evening, but I just wouldn't be good company."

"I never force a lady against her will." He said it lightly, but his annoyance came through.

"Will you give me a rain check?"

"Why not?" He went to the other room and came back with her coat and his.

"You don't need to see me home."

"Whatever you say." He started to go back with the coat.

Norah wavered. It might be better to let him take her home. It would allay his resentment and stop any suspicions from forming later on when he had time to review the evening. She bit her lip. "My husband is . . . a violent man. I wouldn't want . . . anything to happen. But, actually, I'd be grateful if you did see me home. . . . If you wouldn't mind."

Her instincts had been right. Eilbott brightened. As he

154

slipped into his coat, he grinned at her and spoke in a clipped British accent. "Not to worry, luv. I can take care of meself."

Joe had been trying all day to get Norah. He knew it was her day off so he'd given her a little extra time to sleep, but by nine o'clock, when he tried their number, she'd already left. He called at lunchtime, midafternoon, again around six. Where was she? What could she be doing? He tried Mulcahaney, but she wasn't with her father. Around eight Joe decided to go over to the apartment.

There was no answer to his ring, no sound inside. He wasn't anxious, there was no reason to be, but he was disappointed. He had decided that his mother was right, that there was no use waiting for divine intervention to solve his and Norah's problem; they had to do it themselves. He had also acknowledged that he wasn't blameless. He'd complained about the lack of communication, but instead of trying to improve it he'd destroyed what little they had by walking out. He wanted to admit to Norah that he'd been wrong.

Instead he stood uncertainly in front of his own apartment door. He had his key, of course, but he wasn't sure whether or not he should let himself in. He had the right . . . and yet . . . he didn't. That hurt.

He went back down. He left the building, crossed the street, and was starting up the block when he noticed a cab coming around the corner from Madison. There was no reason why he should pay it particular attention, yet instinctively he moved into the nearest doorway. He watched as the cab pulled up in front of their building and a man got out, then handed Norah out. A date. She'd been out on a date. Well, why not? Norah was a beautiful and desirable woman. Joe felt a tightening across his chest as he watched the man, who was very good-looking, escort his wife to the front door. Was she going to ask him up? Thank God he hadn't gone inside to wait. Joe held his breath . . . no, she was sending him away. Without even a friendly good-night kiss! Joe let his breath out slowly, aware of the extent of the strain only by the measure of his present relief.

But though Norah was gone, her date showed no sign of moving on. He stood at the edge of the sidewalk looking up

155

toward the window of the apartment. After a few moments the curtain was pulled aside and Norah appeared. She waved. The man waved back. The curtain fell and finally the man sauntered off.

Joe remained where he was, inside the doorway.

Okay, okay, so Norah had been out on a date. He'd looked up an old girlfriend, hadn't he? The ending of that little incident still brought a glow of embarrassment. Forget it. He couldn't. He hadn't expected Norah to date; it wasn't like her. On the other hand, it couldn't have been much of an evening for her either or she wouldn't have come home this early. Joe felt a lot more cheerful. Also, she hadn't invited the guy up. That tender wave from the window, though . . . he wasn't too crazy about that.

He left the doorway and started across the street toward the house. No. He stopped at the curb. This was not the moment to approach Norah. No. He'd had news for her, too, big news, that he'd been eager to share, but the joy was gone. Another time. He'd tell her about it another time—assuming she still cared.

15

NORAH GOT the information she wanted the next day at the New York Public Library, music and drama branch. The off-off Broadway play in which Leon Eilbott had briefly appeared (five performances) had somehow found a publisher. A quick scanning confirmed what Norah had suspected. There had been other, better known and better rendered versions of the famous case, but *The Grave Robbers* was indeed the story of Dr. Robert Knox of Edinburgh and the trade in corpses for dissection during the early nineteenth century.

At the time, Edinburgh was renowned for its medical schools, but the bodies that anatomists needed for study were hard to come by. Demand created supply, and the doctors' zeal for knowledge spawned a brisk trade in grave robbing. A particularly adept and enterprising pair of grave robbers named Burke and Hare, however, greedy for profit, grew impatient with waiting for the natural death and decent burial of the merchandise. They evolved a method of speeding up the process. Obviously the deaths had to appear natural, both for the sake of the buyer as well as the seller and also to preserve the integrity of the various organs for the subsequent examination. Therefore the victim had to be selected with some care: He had to be alone in the world so that embarrassing questions would not be asked later; he had to be old and weak, preferably made helpless by drink. Having found such a likely prospect, one of the team would throw him to the ground and hold him there by the weight of his own body on the chest, then a hand was placed over nose and mouth and the other hand used to force the lower jaw hard against the upper. The combination caused asphyxiation with almost no trace of trauma. In fact, so expeditious was the method and so nearly undetectable that the unsavory team of Burke and Hare dispatched uncounted numbers of unfortunates before they were apprehended. The method was dubbed "burking" after its initiator and principal practitioner.

Particularly suited to the needs of the time, burking appeared to have little modern application—till now. The grisly case was famous in both medical and legal annals. As an avid reader of everything connected with police work Norah was particularly intrigued by stories of famous cases and trials, had accumulated a surprising amount of forensic and legal knowledge, and was generally familiar with the case. Leon Eilbott knew about it because he had been in a show that told the dreadful story. What Norah knew (though she'd had to refresh her memory by consulting the pertinent section in her *Legal Medicine, Pathology, and Toxicology*) and the actor did not know, however, was that twentieth-century medicine had

157

developed a test by which the nineteenth-century method could be detected and its user convicted.

The next step was to check her theory with Doc Osterman. The ME was intrigued but cautious. She was told that her reconstruction was plausible, certainly, and medically consistent, but her theory for proving it a real long shot. "Always assuming that he used anything other than his bare hands to cut off the victim's air," Osterman reminded her.

"We have to hope that he was too fastidious to use his bare hands," Norah replied. "That being so, I don't think he'd rely on finding something at the scene. He'd bring it with him and take it away again."

"We also have to hope that some saliva escaped from the victim's mouth before he slammed it shut for her."

"Or maybe some mucus from her nostrils. . . ."

Osterman grunted. "Assuming we get enough of the exemplar—saliva or mucus—to permit testing, we come to the biggest hurdle. Was the victim a secretor? There are two types of individuals—those who have the ability to secrete the specific substances by which we can deduce blood type in their tissues and organs and those who do not. If the victim belonged to the group that doesn't secrete, then finding the mucus or the saliva isn't going to do us any good."

Norah refused to be discouraged. "But if she was a secretor and her saliva does yield her blood group, then we've got *him*. How's he going to explain a saliva stain with the victim's blood group on something that belongs to him?"

"Depends on what the something is," Osterman observed tartly. "I'm not saying it's not worth a try, I'm just reminding you that there's a whole chain of conditions to be fulfilled." He paused. "Has it occurred to you that Eilbott might himself be a secretor?"

"Ah, Doc. . . ." Norah was impatient with what she considered his scientific fussiness. "It's no different from testing an ordinary bloodstain to find out if it belongs to the victim or the suspect. You wouldn't argue about the odds then."

"I'm trying to point out the probabilities, but since you apparently already know them, go ahead."

"Asa. . . ."

"Go ahead, Sergeant, go on. Nobody's stopping you." He

158

dropped the receiver back onto the cradle with a clatter that made Norah wince.

By midmorning Norah had her warrant and was ready. She took David with her, choosing him not merely because he'd done the major work on Leon Eilbott but because she still felt most comfortable working with him.

"Do you care whether or not Eilbott knows we've given his place a toss?"

Norah considered. They both knew that the actor would not be at home, that he'd be out on location. "I don't think it matters. As long as he doesn't know what we're looking for."

"What are we looking for?" David asked.

"Something with spit on it."

David gaped at her. "Spit?"

Carefully Norah explained.

If the killer had used an old rag, he would have thrown it away. If he'd used a handkerchief over the victim's nose and mouth, that would have been laundered many times over by now. Norah clung to her faith that having at last discovered the method, they would not now be thwarted in proving it. In fact, she had convinced herself that Leon Eilbott had not used a rag or a handkerchief or even a scarf, but had—quite simply—worn gloves. Wasn't that the simple and logical explanation of the total absence of fingerprints at any of the various crime scenes? So while David went through Leon Eilbott's bureau drawers, Norah examined his closets and almost immediately came on what she'd been hoping and praying to find—a pair of gloves, one of which, the left, showed a scummy stain on the palm. She broke out in a cold sweat, and her knees wobbled with relief. The gloves were quite evidently new, but they'd been stuffed into the pocket of a very old and dilapidated raincoat. The left glove was immediately sent to the lab; the right glove was given to Brennan to trace.

The leather was thin but strong, of fine quality, and the word "Firenze" was stamped on the inside. There weren't that many importers of fine leather gloves in the city and even fewer retail outlets. One of them was an elegant new shop on Seventy-ninth and Columbus Avenue. The owner knew the merchandise; it had sold well. He was perfectly willing to consult his records, though most of the transactions had been cash. When Brennan reported to Norah that Leon Eilbott's name had appeared on a Master Charge voucher for the gloves, she was sure that the breaks were finally going their way. If the stain on the left palm was in fact saliva, the odds were fifty-fifty that it would have the qualities necessary to determine the blood group of the victim. There was nothing to do but wait for the lab report.

Though the job had top priority, it still took time. Norah sat at her desk long after she was off duty waiting for the phone to ring. David didn't go home when he was supposed to either. He said he had other work to do, which undoubtedly he had, but she also knew that the work could have waited. He was staying to keep her company. They sat desks apart, the normal confusion of the squad room between them, yet his presence was a comfort. At one point David made a phone call he didn't want her to know about. The signs were easy to read—wary glances in her direction, turning his back when he spoke and cupping his hand over the mouthpiece. He had to be canceling something he and Marie had planned. Later on, Norah thought, she'd have to thank Marie, let David's wife know that she appreciated the sacrifice of their evening. For now she was just grateful.

At a little after eight Norah's phone rang.

"Homicide, Sergeant Mulcahaney." It was the lab. Her eyes sought David's, and he came right over. "There was sufficient exemplar to conduct the tests? Good, good." She exchanged congratulatory smiles with David. "Did it yield a blood type? . . . Terrific. And. . . ?

She stopped smiling. "You're sure?"

"Well, thanks anyway, Harry. . . . Yeah, I'm sorry, too. I thought the odds were in our favor, but. . . . No, don't bother to call him. I'll talk to Asa in the morning." She hung up.

"What? What happened?"

"The saliva yielded an AB blood type."

It took a couple of seconds before he realized what that meant. "Oh, God. I don't believe it. I just don't believe it."

Norah sighed heavily.

"It was one hell of a good idea, Norah. We could have nailed him."

160

"Sure."

"Those are the breaks, kid." He rested a hand on her shoulder. "Well, we'll just have to come up with something else."

Norah nodded, but she had no such hope. She was discouraged, depleted, wrung out. She had agonized over this case, twisted and turned the facts looking for the loophole and had been convinced that she'd finally found it. As each link in the chain of her reasoning was validated, she became more confident. Induction was proved fact. To fail now, at the very end, was that much more disheartening. The irony of it was that the final lab test did not invalidate the preceding evidence. It did not exonerate Leon Eilbott. It didn't say he hadn't committed the crimes; it merely failed to provide proof that he did.

The test had successfully identified the saliva stain on Eilbott's glove and extracted the victim's blood group from it—type AB. AB is the rarest group. Only three to five percent of the population have it. Grace Swann had it. Unfortunately, according to his military record, so did Leon Eilbott.

The odds against their both having AB blood were twenty to one.

The first thing Norah did the next morning when she got to work was call Asa Osterman. As usual, the ME was fatalistic; it really had been too much to expect, too much of a long shot. He really wasn't surprised.

But she wouldn't give up, not yet. "Wasn't there some way to differentiate within the same blood group?"

"Sure," Osterman replied. "Any number of ways. There are M, N, MN subdivisions. There are Rh factors and Kell-Cellano factors. Any of them would differentiate the blood of the victim from that of the suspect despite their being of the same major group. There's just one problem: Only a sample of the blood itself will yield the information—not the saliva."

Norah was silent.

"There is one possibility."

She perked up.

"I did mention to you that Eilbott might be a secretor. Suppose he's a nonsecretor."

161

She gasped. "I forgot. How could I forget? That's it, Doc, that's it!"

"Of course, in order to find out, you've got to get me some exemplar. A used handkerchief if it has some mucus on it would do. Even a cigarette stub might yield enough."

"He doesn't smoke. I'll check his laundry...." She had been riffling through the messages on her desk. One caught her eye; it concerned Eilbott. He had called to protest the invasion of his apartment. "I should have done it while I was there." She slammed her fist hard on the desk top. "I goofed. Oh, blessed Virgin, how I goofed!"

"Hell, it was up to me to warn you to pick up something of the suspect's just in case," Osterman soothed.

"You tried, Asa; I wouldn't listen. I was just too eager and too sure of myself. As usual," she added bitterly.

Osterman cleared his throat. "It happens to all of us sometimes; why should you be any different? So forget it. Think of something else. You can do it."

"Thanks, Asa," Norah murmured, but the tough little man, ashamed of having shown that much sentiment, had already hung up.

So. Norah heaved a sigh and gave a desultory look at the rest of the message. Eilbott's call had been referred to Brennan, and Roy had told the actor that if he wanted further information he'd have to contact the officer in charge. He hadn't given Norah's name, and Eilbott, who was leaving for Hollywood momentarily, had been too preoccupied to ask. He had assured Brennan, however, that when he got back the officer would be hearing from him. It was the least of Norah's troubles.

For Norah the elderly, defenseless, and trusting victims of Eilbott's assembly-line murders had become symbols of all the pathetic old people who were daily assaulted in all kinds of ways—some of them legal. She felt that by avenging these eight women she would be avenging the others, at least serving notice that they could not be violated with impunity. Of course she would manage somehow to get hold of a sample of Eilbott's saliva. Assuming that the test results were favorable, she realized now that it might not be enough to convince a jury—even in conjunction with the burking MO. She

162

wanted Eilbott brought to trial with as little chance of acquittal as possible.

The actor was due back in a week. He had assured Brennan that he would then look up the officer who had searched his apartment. Innocent, his indignation was warranted; guilty, he had to go through the motions. The confrontation was inevitable. Norah wondered how she might use it.

It doesn't take much to disrupt a shooting schedule: a star's temperament, illness or accident, from trivia to cataclysm, the delays are legendary. They can bring even a major studio to the edge of bankruptcy and certainly wipe out an independent. Director Stanislas Sadler was the darling of the television film industry for his ability to maintain a tight schedule and thus bring in his pictures comfortably under the limit. It was certainly unusual for Sadler to require retakes, particularly on location. Of course, going back to New York wasn't all that expensive; he could work with a local crew, and both the leading actors, Leon Eilbott and Linda Turner, were from New York and their return fare had to be paid anyway.

The location was to be Rockefeller Center, specifically the sunken plaza, an area dear to the hearts of filmmakers because it was so recognizably *New York*. The whole thing would be handled with a minimum of fuss. The camera would be concealed in a doorway and camouflaged with heavy padding so that only the lens remained uncovered and the casual passerby would not even be aware that there was anything unusual going on. Sadler's reputation for economy suited Norah's purpose, for she wasn't particularly eager to attract attention either. The choice of scene was close to ideal: It was almost completely self-enclosed and would require only a couple of men to block the stairs leading down from the promenade and a couple more at the doorways at substreet level; her people could also mix in with the public unobtrusively. Of course, Rockefeller Center is private property, but the center's public relations office lived up to its reputation for sympathy and cooperation, and as it was between seasons— the skating rink having closed and the outdoor restaurant not yet opened—they readily granted a shooting permit.

Even the weather assisted in restoring Stanislas Sadler's

reputation for bringing in a picture on schedule. At eight A.M. on the Saturday the temperature was sixty-three degrees and expected to hit close to eighty; humidity comfortable; sun mellow in a clear sky; breeze just enough to ruffle the tender new green of the street trees. The stores along Fifth Avenue were fresh and bright with their Easter displays. It was as though the avenue had put on its best face to be photographed, Norah thought as she walked from the bus stop. She had planned the coming interview in detail, outlined it on paper, and learned the points she must cover. Experience, however, had taught her not to fix herself too rigidly, but to leave some flexibility and to be ready to receive impressions and insights so that she could take advantage of unexpected opportunities. As a rule she made it a practice to clear her mind before an important interrogation. But today it was more difficult than usual. There was a bad traffic jam in front of St. Patrick's Cathedral. A fleet of buses had lined up and were unloading passengers. Horns blared, drivers shouted, pedestrians jostled one another as they dodged between cars to cross the intersection. Norah hardly noticed. She had just been informed that the Senior Citizens Squad was to be terminated.

Jim Felix had assured her that it was purely an economy measure; as such, it was hardly unexpected. The city had been in crisis for a long time. Wave after wave of firings had shaken the department. With men uncertain about whether they would have a job, and the city uncertain about whether it could pay those who had, she could not protest. Still, she was depressed. Today was the last day of the unit's existence and her last day as its head. She was determined to wrap up the case so that it would go on record as having been solved by the unit. She wanted them both to go out big. She squared her shoulders, thrust out her chin, and turned the corner into the Rockefeller Center Promenade.

It was still too early for more than a handful of shoppers to be peering into windows or tourists to be out sightseeing, and that was all to the good. Norah walked purposefully past the display of tulips and dogwood trees toward the stairs that led into the sunken plaza. Augie Baum leaned idly against the parapet smoking a cigarette; Gus Schmidt was apparently lost

164

in contemplation of a display of men's haberdashery. Neither so much as glanced at her as she passed. She paused to check the disposition of the film people and her unit below. Sadler and the cameraman were to the left of the golden statue of Prometheus, the camera itself set up in the doorway of the French restaurant. She spotted Brennan and Link among the men surrounding the director. Link looked up. Norah squinted and raised her hand to shield her eyes.

Just then Sadler called out, "Okay, people. Let's go."

Eilbott stepped out of the shadows behind the statue and joined the director for instructions. With him was the girl who'd worked in the scene at the park a week earlier. After a brief consultation they separated, taking positions on opposite sides of the concealed camera. The handful of people involved were quiet and alert; the public on the street above went about its business unconcerned. At a nod from Sadler, Eilbott moved forward into camera range, looking in the direction of the girl. He waved to her and started to speak and the shriek of a fire engine seemed to come right out of his mouth.

"Cut, cut!" Sadler called. "Damn," he muttered.

Nobody was very excited; it was the kind of thing you got used to on location.

Sadler only shrugged as the wailing and clanging grew louder; evidently more than one engine was passing. For the first time the director seemed to notice the young actress. "Say, honey, is that what wardrobe gave you for this scene? It's wrong. Completely out of character. We've got to find you something else. Come on." He led her into the restaurant.

This was the moment Norah had been waiting for. She started down the stairs and approached Eilbott.

"Hi."

"Norah! Well, Norah . . . this is a surprise. I didn't expect to see you." He grinned. "Come to see if our permits are in order and if everybody's happy?"

"Not this time."

"Oh? What are you doing here?"

"I came to see you."

"Really? That's an unexpected pleasure."

"You asked to see me. You called the precinct and said you

165

wanted to talk to the officer responsible for searching your apartment. That's me."

He gaped. "You're a police officer? You're putting me on."

Delving into her handbag, Norah brought out her ID and held it open for him to see. "Okay?"

"Sergeant Mulcahaney." He read the name, looked at the picture, then looked at Norah. "Mulcahaney," he repeated.

"Ring a bell?" she asked.

"You came back to my apartment the next day?" he wanted to know.

"With a warrant."

"That was a lousy thing to do. I mean the act you put on—all that talk about your husband, how scared of him you were, how nervous about his seeing us together. And I swallowed it. I fell for it all."

"My husband and I are separated; I told you the truth about that. The rest was your idea."

"You didn't tell me I was wrong. You let me go on thinking it. Anyhow"—he dismissed that with a wave of his hand—"let's get to the point, Sergeant Mulcahaney. Why are you so interested in me? I assume this visit isn't any more social than the first one was. So what do you want?"

"First, I have to inform you of your rights." Norah began the official recitation. "You have the right to remain—"

"This comes a little late, doesn't it? Shouldn't you have gone through this a week ago? You're not from the mayor's film office and you never were. You lied. You tried to set me up and you used your sex to do it."

She'd never been accused of that before. Norah flushed. "I only meant to observe you. You asked me for a date."

"And you accepted. You came into my home as a friend. You snooped around under false pretenses. You're not supposed to do that," he accused, shoulders hunched, face drawn, mouth in a straight hard line. Then, all at once, he changed.

"Oh, hell, Norah, I'm sorry." He gave her that special, engaging, and, this time, slightly aggrieved smile. "I don't mean to blow up at you, but it is quite a shock to find out that the pretty woman I was trying to make time with is a police

166

officer, not only that but a police officer investigating me." His eyes pleaded. "What am I supposed to have done, Norah?

Could it really be that her name meant nothing to him? Was it possible that he didn't know? Well, for now she had to play it his way. "You may remember a while back, in late November, there was a lot of publicity about several unexplained deaths in an apartment hotel called the Westvue."

"I think so." He frowned. "Sure. Didn't some kid confess?"

"He didn't do it."

"Oh? So? Wait a minute, wait a minute! I know who you are. I've got you now. You're the lady detective who stumbled on the whole hornet's nest. You got your husband—a lieutenant —fired. . . . But I thought the police claimed the deaths were natural. As I recall the newspaper stories, the medical examiner insisted there was no foul play. That was your husband's defense."

He talked as though Joe were on trial, Norah thought, but she refused to rise to the bait. It was a good act, very good, and she must keep reminding herself that acting was his business. "We've since uncovered other deaths that fit the same pattern."

For a moment he showed surprise, but covered it quickly. "I should think that would make your husband's position worse."

Norah ignored that. "Each victim died by suffocation. Each victim was a female, elderly, living alone. Each one died on the third day of the month. Each one was on Social Security and on the third of the month received her check, which she then cashed at the Federated Check-Cashing Service on Broadway. You used to work for Federated."

"Oh, for God's sake, is that what this is all about?" He seemed both relieved and angry. "Why didn't you say so? You could have saved us both a lot of time and anxiety. I quit Federated over a year ago."

"You quit on January eleventh because you got a job in a Broadway show."

He raised an eyebrow. "Right."

"The show folded out of town, in Philadelphia. Six weeks after you quit Federated, you tried to get your old job back.

167

But the manager wasn't having you. He was mad as hell at you for leaving without notice and he swore he'd never hire another actor again."

"Okay, that's true. So what?"

"So you didn't get work till August that year when you were in an industrial show that lasted another six weeks. January of this year you did a TV commercial. This is your only other job. How have you been living?"

"You already asked me that."

"And you told me that your family helps you out."

He shrugged. "Okay, so I lied. But they used to help me out."

"Answer the question."

"I play the numbers. I'm lucky at the track. I don't have to tell you where I get my money. It's none of your business."

"It is if you killed eight defenseless old women to get it."

"Eight!"

"That's how many we've discovered so far. Were there more?"

"God! Norah . . . do you honestly believe that I did such a thing? I know we've only spent a couple of hours together, but even in that short time I sensed a rapport between us. If you believe me capable of this . . . then I guess I was wrong." He sighed. "Why pick on me? Why don't you go hassle the other employees at Federated?"

"They have alibis."

"Maybe I do, too. Why don't you ask me? Why don't you tell me the times involved and I'll—"

"Try to come up with something? I don't think you can, but it's not important. You see, none of the other employees of Federated can be presumed to have any knowledge of burking."

He paled at that. Despite the layer of makeup, Norah could see the color drain out of his face. His eyes narrowed speculatively; the tip of his tongue licked at the cleft in his upper lip. "You saw the picture on my wall, so there's no use denying that I know what you're talking about. Sure, I know about burking and so does every other actor and stagehand and usher and cleaning woman connected with the show. And everybody in the audience that came to see it."

168

"None of them worked for Federated."

"You can't make a case out of that. That's a coincidence!" he roared, then he made another of those complete reversals. "You know what I think, Norah, luv? I think you're on a fishing expedition. I don't believe you have a single damn thing on me."

"Actually, we do have a very strong circumstantial case against you, Leon." She had reached a crossroads. There were two ways the interrogation could go: She could try to trick Eilbott, but she didn't think he'd fall for it and if he did, his lawyer might later charge entrapment. She decided to play it straight. "We know that you're guilty. The trouble is we can't prove it."

Eilbott frowned. As an actor he was trained to transmit meaning by the most subtle inflection, the most imperceptible of gestures, so he also knew how to interpret such signs in others. He knew that Norah was telling the truth; what he couldn't fathom was why she'd made the admission.

"What's more, you know that we can't prove it," Norah said casually, almost carelessly. "But we came close. You have no idea how close." She permitted herself a fleeting sigh.

Eilbott's eyes never left her face.

"I don't mind telling you," Norah went on, "our main obstacle is proving that murder was committed at all. And that, of course, is what you're depending on—that we can't prove it. I'm sure that once you discovered burking, you thought you had an undetectable murder method. But medicine has advanced since the days when it was necessary to buy corpses from grave robbers for medical study. For instance, we know now that all blood is not the same, not even human blood. There are several distinct groupings."

Despite himself, Eilbott nodded like an earnest student at a lecture.

"Everybody knows that it's a relatively simple matter to determine to which group a person belongs, but did you know it doesn't require a sample of the actual blood to do it? It doesn't. The blood group can be determined by the analysis of other body secretions. The saliva, for example." She paused to give him a chance not only to assimilate that but perhaps to anticipate what was coming.

169

"Since we found no unexplained fingerprints at any of the scenes of the suspected homicides, we reasoned that the killer wore gloves. It was possible that when he placed his gloved hand over the victim's nose and mouth, some of her saliva might have trickled out and stained the glove. That's what we were looking for when we searched your place, Leon—the gloves you wore when you killed those women and, we hoped, one victim's spittle on the palm."

Eilbott remained transfixed.

"We did find the gloves," she informed him. "And the stain, too."

They had both forgotten time and place. Certainly they were not aware that the fire engines that had disrupted the shooting had long since passed out of earshot. Nobody came near to tell them.

"We thought it didn't matter which of your victims' saliva was on the glove, but we were wrong. The saliva was Grace Swann's. Her blood group is AB."

It took Leon Eilbott several seconds to grasp the significance. "I'm AB."

"Yes, I know, but she was a secretor; you may not be."

He looked sick. He turned away, shoulders shaking so that Norah thought he was going to throw up. After a few moments he faced her again, pale and grim, but in control.

"If you think I'm going to submit to any cockamamy tests, forget it."

"Up to you." Norah shrugged. She opened her handbag, took out a handkerchief, and wiped her face.

"Okay, people, we're back in business," Stanislas Sadler announced.

Eilbott started to take his place.

"Where do you think you're going?" Norah asked. "You're not going to be playing any scenes for a while."

He gaped at her. "But . . . but you just said—"

"I said the saliva test was inconclusive. I didn't say I wouldn't arrest you." She opened her handbag and this time brought out a pair of handcuffs.

He stared at the handcuffs, then at her. "I don't believe this. I don't believe any of this. You mean you're not going to let me do the scene? You can't stop me."

"Try me."

"But why? What's the point? It's crazy. The whole thing is crazy. You said yourself you don't have any real evidence. You have to arrest me to protect your job, is that it?"

"I should warn you that I'm not here alone, Leon. There are detectives covering the area—working with the crew, in the restaurants, on the stairs."

He didn't even bother to look where she pointed. "I don't care how many men you've got, I'm playing the scene. You'll have to carry me away to stop me."

"We can do that."

"You mean it, don't you? You really mean it?" He sighed. "Norah, don't you understand what this scene means? I'm not asking just for myself. If I don't do the scene, the picture won't be finished and that's going to hurt everybody—the other actors, the designers, writers, producers. . . ."

"I'm sorry."

"Sorry isn't good enough! Norah, please!" He clasped his hands in earnest appeal. "Please, let me do the scene. How long is it going to take? A few minutes, a quarter of an hour at most. I know you have no feeling for me, that the feeling is all on my side, but what's a quarter of an hour to you? For me it's my whole professional career. I've waited so long. I've sacrificed so much. I can't get away. Where can I go?" Looking around to emphasize the point, the actor seemed at last aware that escape was effectively blocked. "If you don't let me play this scene and finish the picture, they'll get somebody else. They'll replace me. They'll throw out all my footage and reshoot. It'll be expensive but they won't have any choice."

"I imagine they'll wait a few days before doing anything that drastic. You'll be released by then, if you're innocent."

His eyes held on her for a long time.

"Well, we both know it'll be more than a few days before I'm released. You're a smart lady, a real smart lady." He took a step toward her, and despite her best efforts, Norah flinched. "Okay, what's the idea? What do you want? A confession? Okay, I'll confess."

He had taken the bait! Norah sucked in her breath and felt the clammy, cold, nervous goose bumps break out all over. Just how deep in was the hook? She probed.

171

"You could deny it all later," she told him. "No, thanks, I've been that route before. I'm taking you in."

He froze. His face was pale, muscles rigid. After a moment he glanced over his shoulder toward the concealed camera and the waiting crew, then back to Norah.

She'd read him right, Norah thought. He'd counted on a one-on-one situation, her word against his. She could have got herself wired, of course, but she didn't want to be accused of trickery or entrapment. Quietly, almost soothingly, as though offering a solution, she murmured, "I have a tape recorder."

"Oh? Well. . . ." He hesitated.

Was he figuring the odds on beating a taped confession? Norah wondered. Leon Eilbott was a man obsessed. He saw this movie as his chance for fame. He had come down a long road to this moment, sacrificed so many women to his monomania, his white whale. Norah was gambling that he wouldn't, or couldn't, stop now.

"Okay," he said suddenly. "Okay. Let's get the show on the road."

For just a second Norah's eyes closed and she permitted herself a soft sigh of relief, then she took the little machine out of her bag. "You're making this confession of your own free will?"

"Yes, yes, absolutely. What do you want me to say?"

He was so eager. She had the impression of an actor in the wings impatient to make his entrance. "I want the truth."

"Really? Really, Sergeant Mulcahaney?" He thought that having made a deal, he had a right to arrogance. "I don't believe that. I've been trying to figure your stake in this. You got your husband into hot water over this case and it looks to me like everything you've done since is making it worse. Maybe you don't care, but if you're interested in repairing the damage, I'm willing to help. I'll get your husband off the hook. I'll say whatever you want me to say. I'll confess or deny whatever you tell me to."

It was an outrageous suggestion, of course, but for a moment, just one, Norah allowed herself to think about what it could mean for Joe and for her . . . and was shocked at how tempted she was.

"No."

172

"No what?"

"No deal." She was even more shocked at the regret.

"Than what the hell are you after?" he shouted.

"The truth. The truth, whatever it may be. I want to know exactly what you did and didn't do."

"I could pile it on, you know. Really fix your husband. Make him look like a bum . . . and you, too."

She had herself in hand again. "Why should you?"

"To get even."

"I'll take the chance."

"How do I know that you'll keep your part of the bargain? How do I know that after I tell you what you want you'll let me play the scene? How do I know you won't march me right off to jail?"

What could she tell him? How could she convince him? "I didn't have to tell you the truth about the saliva test. I could have let you think the results proved you guilty."

Slowly Eilbott nodded. Again he looked toward the hidden camera, then at Stanislas Sadler. He swallowed.

"Give me a couple of minutes, will you, Stan?" he called, then drew back into the shadow of the statue.

Norah followed, held up the recorder, and flipped the switch again. A contemplative look came over his face as he addressed himself to the machine.

"I think the first thing I want to say is that I never intended to hurt any of the poor old things. I didn't want them to suffer, not even for a second, if I could help it. And that is the God's truth. Actually, I was very sorry for them. They were waiting to die. I did them a favor. I put an end to their waiting."

For Norah the logic behind a murder always exerted a dreadful fascination. What was particularly appalling to her in this instance was that Eilbott really had pitied his victims. She wanted to hear no more of that. "Start with the women at the Westvue. Phoebe Laifer. If she was the first?"

He appeared lost in thought.

"She was a writer of children's books. Manually strangled."

"Yes, yes, I know. I remember." He was irritated at being prompted. It was as though he were playing a scene and a line had been thrown to him when he didn't need it. "I was sorry

173

about her. She struggled. She was a lot stronger than I had anticipated. I couldn't hold her down long enough to cut off her air with my hands. She bit me. Here, here, look—you can still see the mark."

By this time the scar had almost disappeared, but it loomed still raw in Eilbott's sight because he remembered the pain, and in Norah's because she could visualize the victim's desperation.

"It was after that that I started wearing gloves."

A much better reason than Norah had come up with and a detail which would help authenticate the confession.

"She bit me, and naturally I pulled my hand away. As soon as I did that, she started to yell. I had to shut her up. I really had no choice. I bungled the whole thing," Eilbott admitted. "To start with, Miss Laifer was a bad choice. I was more careful in my next selection, and then, too, my technique improved."

Norah was revolted.

He caught her look. "When I say that Miss Laifer was a mistake, I don't mean because she put up such a fight, but because she was still productive. The others were not only unwanted, friendless, but they had long since stopped fulfilling any useful function. Their lives had no meaning. I gave meaning to their dying. To each one I explained my ambition and my dedication. I told each one about my dear mother. How she'd been a promising young actress and had given up her career to bear me and to raise me. How I felt obliged to succeed for her sake. How I'd promised her on her deathbed that I would never give up. I asked for their help and they were glad to give it. Each one was glad for me to have the money."

Sure, Norah thought, sure. The terrified victim had been only too eager to put the money in his hands, thinking thereby to buy her life. "Let's get on to victim number two: Bernice Hoysradt. She was suffocated by a gag stuffed too far down her windpipe."

"She had no strength at all. After Miss Laifer I expected more resistance. I only brought the gag to prevent her screaming, and I guess I forced it down too hard. I was still new at it."

174

Norah hurried on. "Estelle Waggoner."

He frowned. "I don't remember her."

"She was stabbed."

"No. I never stabbed anybody. I wouldn't do that. I told you, I tried to make it as easy as possible for them."

"Mrs. Waggoner was seventy-seven years old, blond, she'd been in vaudeville."

"A performer? I wouldn't take money from another performer. Never."

"You couldn't know her past history."

"After Miss Laifer I made it a point to find out as much as I could about them. I sort of arranged to run into them and talk a little before the final decision."

"So that when you rang the doorbell you were no stranger. They weren't afraid to let you in. Mrs. Swann even served you tea. In her best china," Norah added bitterly.

He flushed at that, as though he'd been accused of a breach of etiquette.

Norah sighed. "You're sure about Estelle Waggoner?"

"I never stabbed anybody. I never took money from another performer. I did take money from Miss Laifer and that little bony Miss Hoysradt and Mrs. Swann. There were, I think . . . four others . . . I think. I'm not sure. I'm sorry, I can't seem to remember. Suddenly I can't remember them individually. It was so easy, you see, after the first two or three. But I should remember. I owe them remembrance. I owe them that." He appeared both confused and distressed. "I do know that I was as gentle as I could be with each one. I didn't spill blood." Then, to prove that he was telling the truth, he added, "I can't stand the sight of blood."

Norah shuddered. She had never been completely satisfied with Doc Osterman's theory that the killer had been experimenting with various MO's. Floundering, yes, but always within the same style.

"So how about it, Norah?" Eilbott broke into her reverie. "Can we shoot now?"

"What? Oh, yes, sure. Go ahead."

He metamorphosed before her eyes—from a loser he became a winner. Shoulders back, stomach in, head tilted at an insouciant angle, he strolled to his position in front of the

175

camera. "Sorry to have kept you all waiting," he announced, then called to the director, "Do we need another run-through, Stan? Why don't we make this one a take?"

"If you think you're ready, Leon, sure."

"I'm ready."

"Okay. Quiet on the set. Quiet, please. This is a take."

Within the silence there was an uneasy stirring. David Link slipped to Norah's side. "You think this is a good idea?"

"I promised." She shrugged. "Where can he go? What can he do?"

"Action."

Aware that everyone's eyes were on him, the actor began to play his part. He walked slowly and deliberately into camera range, waved to the girl, speaking softly for the boom mike alone. Then Eilbott turned and looked directly into the lens, holding the pose for what Norah supposed would be a close-up.

"Cut! Cut and print," Sadler announced with considerable satisfaction. "Nice work, Leon. Nice work, everybody. Thank you."

On the instant, the job of packing up began. Not that there was much to it, just the stripping of the camouflage from the camera, dismantling it and the sound equipment. Sadler and the actress scurried out of the way, but Leon Eilbott seemed to be in some kind of trance. Standing in place, he was jostled and shoved—his moment in the spotlight over.

"Look at him, David," Norah murmured. "He looks lost, confused; he's a totally different person now that the scene is over. What is he? Some kind of schizophrenic? A psycho? What?"

"He's a killer," the detective replied coldly, without compassion. "A homicidal maniac. Let's get him."

Leon Eilbott smiled when he saw them coming and backed off a couple of steps. He had his own script to follow. "Where are the rest of your people?" he asked Norah. "I don't see all those detectives. Where's the fuzz? Where are you?" he called in his most booming actor's voice, and looked around the sunken plaza and up at the pedestrians along the promenade. "Come out, come out, wherever you are!"

Baum and Schmidt instantly ran down and took positions at the foot of the stairs. Brennan, dropping all pretense of working with the crew, moved to within a couple of feet of Eilbott. Arenas materialized on his other side.

"That's better." Eilbott nodded approvingly and, before either Norah or Link could make a move, jumped up to the parapet around the statue's base as though he were leaping up on a stage.

Whereas she had been anxious to attract as little attention as possible, attention was what Eilbott wanted, Norah realized.

"Come and get me!" he yelled gleefully.

Instantly the detectives formed a half circle in front of him, guns drawn. Everybody else scattered—fast. Once again Leon Eilbott was the center of attention.

The actor smiled broadly.

"That's more like it," he said. "Okay, here's the way we're going to play it." He pointed to Norah. "On cue, you, Sergeant Mulcahaney, will step forward and put the cuffs on me. As soon as you hear the click, you two"—he indicated Brennan and Link—"will fall in on either side of us. Then you"—he indicated Schmidt and Baum—"in front, with you"—Arenas—"in the rear. When we're all formed up, we'll march past the camera and up the stairs." He frowned. "What are you waiting for?" he demanded of the cameraman. "Set up the shot."

The cameraman hesitated.

"Set up the shot," Eilbott snarled.

"What the hell!" David Link grunted and started forward, but Norah put a hand out to hold him back.

"We'll do it his way."

"Quiet!" Eilbott called. "Quiet on the set. Everybody stay where you are," he ordered.

It wasn't necessary; everybody was frozen in place.

"Action. Come on, Norah."

And Norah did as she'd been instructed, and so did everybody else.

"They won't dare replace me now," Eilbott murmured in her ear as they passed the camera. "This will be terrific publicity for the picture." There was a demonic light in his eyes as he added, "The trial will be even better."

By the time she was through with the arraignment and got back to the precinct it was nearly five o'clock. Norah was

177

exhausted, which was natural, and depressed, which was not. Part of the reason she felt so low was the letdown inevitable at the end of a long, hard investigation and the disbanding of the unit, but principally it was because she hadn't heard from Joe. Not a word. All day. No matter how he felt about their personal relationship, no matter what decision he might have reached, she had certainly expected he would call and offer congratulations.

She got them from every man and woman in the squad room—even Augie Baum. In fact, her entrance caused a mild stir. It was a momnet to be remembered, incomplete because among the sheaf of messages on her desk there was none from Joe. Was it possible that he didn't know what had happened? Hardly. News like this was picked up and passed along the grapevine almost at the instant it happened. If he hadn't called by now, he wasn't going to.

Norah slumped into her chair, propped elbows on the desk, and buried her face in her hands. It was over then. Finished. And yet, it didn't hurt as much as she'd expected. Probably she was too tired to feel the hurt. Tomorrow it would hit her. But by tomorrow she'd already have started getting used to the idea that she and Joe were through. In fact, she was used to it already. Hadn't she been getting used to it these past weeks? She'd survive; she'd adjust. Marriages broke up all the time, every day of the week, and nobody died of it. The only thing was she never imagined it could happen to her and Joe. It would have been nice if they could have stayed friends, but that wasn't in his temperament. She'd get used to that, too.

She got up, set her chin, and walked out of the squad room without a word to anyone. As she closed the door behind her, she heard the ringing of her phone—at least it sounded like her phone. She paused for a moment. All phones sound alike. She was off duty. Let someone else answer.

This was one night when Norah didn't want to be alone. She needed companionship. She thought of calling her father, but the situation with Eileen Fitzgerald was still awkward. Dolly Dollinger was on duty. Of course, she could call David and Marie. In fact, David had suggested she dine with them, but their happiness would be too sharp a reminder of what she was losing. Then she thought of Signora Emilia and felt an unfamiliar need for an older woman's comfort. Odd Fridays had been the days that she and Joe had visited his mother, and she supposed that he had been keeping to the regular schedule during the separation. Today, being Saturday, it was not likely she'd run into him.

Signora Emilia took one look at her daughter-in-law standing forlornly on her threshold and embraced her.

"*Figlia mia*, how happy I am to see you. Are you all right? I heard all about it on the six o'clock news. What an experience!" She peered past Norah into the hall. "Where is Joe? Parking the car?"

"He's not with me."

Signora Emilia's face darkened.

"I don't know where he is. I haven't heard from him all day." She hadn't meant to say anything about that. "Maybe I shouldn't have come?"

"You are my daughter; nothing can change that," Signora Emilia replied firmly, drawing Norah into the apartment. Then she led her into the living room, where she looked her over. "I can tell that you have not eaten, *cara*. So, I am at this moment preparing *gnocchi alla romana*. How does that appeal to you? With plenty of butter and fresh *parmigiano*?"

"It sounds delicious, Mamma, but I'm not really hungry."

"Because you are tired. So, you will go into the bedroom and rest for half an hour—it will take that long for the *gnocchi* to be ready. Then you will eat a double portion."

"I could use a little rest. Are you sure you don't mind, Mamma?"

"Come." Signora Emilia simply took Norah's hand and led her to the bedroom. At the door she stopped. "He did not even telephone you?"

"Maybe he hasn't heard."

According to Signora Capretto, once an event made the six o'clock news it wasn't possible for anyone not to be aware of it. For Norah's sake, she didn't say so. It cost her a prodigious amount of willpower to remain silent and was an indication of how highly she'd come to regard her son's wife. She gave Norah a slight push into the room, then quietly closed the door on her.

179

It was still daylight when Norah pulled back the chenille coverlet of Signora Emilia's bed, took off her shoes, and lay down. When she awoke it was dark. She didn't need to look at her watch to know that she'd slept much longer than the agreed-on half hour. She yawned, sat up, reached under the fringed shade of the bedside lamp for the pull chain. The first thing she saw was the bedside clock. Ten thirty. She bounced to her feet. Signora Emilia shouldn't have let her sleep this late. Hastily Norah slipped into her shoes, straightened her sweater down over her hips, ran a comb through her hair, and opened the bedroom door.

"Mamma? Mamma! I'm up. Where are you?" She went into the living room.

Joe stood by the window.

She felt groggy from the nap; she knew her eyes were puffy and her clothes rumpled. She wished she'd taken the time to wash her face, at least to put on some lipstick.

"I wish your mother hadn't sent for you."

Joe thought she'd never looked more beautiful.

"She didn't. I phoned her. Not that I expected you to be here, but I hoped she might have heard from you. I'd tried everywhere else. I just missed you at the precinct. I called you at home several times. I figured you must be out for dinner, so I waited and then tried again. I spoke to your father. He thought I should go over."

"To the apartment?"

He nodded. "But I didn't think so. I mean, I didn't want to just barge in on you. . . ."

Norah looked questioning.

"In case you . . . in case you had somebody over . . . visiting. Dolly or somebody."

She didn't understand his embarrassment. "That was very considerate."

"But I was starting to worry about you."

Now she got the drift and suddenly felt a lot better. "Why?"

"Well. . . ." He shrugged. "David said you were going straight home." It implied the question, Why didn't you?

Jealous! Joe was jealous. How wonderful! "I changed my mind." Norah tossed it off lightly, let him suffer, just a little.

180

She had no intention of saying more, but somehow it slipped out. "There was nothing to go home to."

"I know."

He'd been lonely, too. Norah's hopes rose further.

"As I said before, I was getting worried, so I decided to call Mamma as a last resort before. . . ."

"Before what?"

"I don't know. I don't know what I would have done if I hadn't found you." His face was drawn, his body tense in the remembrance of his anxiety. Then he relaxed and was his usual easygoing self. "Of course, as soon as I heard Mamma's voice I knew you were here. She wouldn't admit it, though. When I arrived, would you believe she wasn't going to let me in?"

Norah put a hand over her mouth to hide her smile.

"She wouldn't believe that I was tied up all day and didn't have a chance to contact you."

"I don't either."

He sighed. "Okay, you're both right. The truth is I was kind of hoping you'd call me."

Norah's eyes widened. "I never thought of it. I waited all day and it never occurred to me. . . ." The old female conditioning: The man calls first; the man is the pursuer. In this instance, though. . . . "You were the one who walked out."

"I wasn't sure you wanted to hear from me."

"That's ridiculous! How could you possibly think I didn't want to hear from you?"

He hesitated. "I saw you come in from your date the other night."

"What date?"

"How many dates have you had?"

"None."

"Norah, please. I know you've been dating somebody. I told you, I saw the two of you arrive home."

"What are you talking about? When?"

"A couple of weeks ago. In fact, exactly two weeks ago tonight."

She shook her head.

"I was standing right there, Norah! I was right across the

181

street from the house, in the doorway of the florist's shop. I saw the cab pull up; I saw the two of you get out, and I saw the way he said good night to you." With an edge of bitterness, he added, "I also saw you come to the window and wave to him."

Now she knew what he meant. Now she wanted to laugh with relief and joy, to tell him how unfounded his suspicions were, except that she recalled Eilbott's suggesting that her husband was keeping watch on her. "What were you doing in the doorway of the florist's? Were you checking up on me?"

"I was not. I just happened to be passing by and I noticed the cab." He took a deep breath. "That's not true. I was coming to see you."

"You were? Oh, Joe. . . ." It was her turn to be honest. "That was no date. That man was the suspect. That was Leon Eilbott. I'd been over to his. . . ." Too late. She tried to fix it. "Uh . . . I'd been interrogating him . . . sort of. . . ."

"You'd been interrogating a mass murderer . . . sort of? And he brought you home in a cab? Then you went to the window to wave him good-bye? That's an unusual relationship between a detective and a suspect, isn't it? Where did this 'sort of' interrogation take place?"

Norah winced. "Ah . . . in his apartment. But he didn't know I was a police officer." That hadn't helped either.

Joe was aghast. "I don't care whether he knew or not. You knew. You knew or had good reason to suspect what he was. You knew the risk involved."

With all the good intention of admitting her fault and accepting the reprimand, Norah had to defend herself. "That's the point: I was aware of the risk. I was prepared."

Joe was not assuaged. "It was foolhardy. Irresponsible. What's more, it was contrary to procedure. You know better. The only time you walk into that kind of situation is when you've got a backup."

"Yes, Joe."

"Look, I'm not chewing you out just because you're my wife. I'd say the same thing to any officer who pulled that kind of stunt, and you know that. Suppose Eilbott had made you. It could have blown the whole case."

"Yes, Joe. It won't happen again."

182

"Till the next time. I suppose I'll have to learn to live with it."

Norah's hopes soared; she waited expectantly.

But he returned to the lecture. "I'm not saying you didn't do a good job. You did. I'm proud of you. The investigation was first-rate. The psychology behind the interrogation was good; you had him figured just right. I'm not crazy about the location, but I realize you had no choice."

"We would have preferred to do it inside a studio, naturally," Norah admitted. "But then logically it would have had to be done in Hollywood, and then how would I explain my presence?"

"Hold it. Wait a minute. . . ." Joe thought it out very carefully before speaking. "The whole thing was a setup? They didn't need any retakes? The picture was complete?"

"Oh, sure. I thought you knew."

"No, I didn't. Nobody told me. Nobody told me that." A new possibility now occurred to Joe and it made him gasp and at the same time glare at Norah. "You didn't just go ahead. . . ?"

"On my own? Of course not! I used to do things like that when I was a rookie; I know better now." The twinkle in her eyes belied the indignation; Norah was enjoying herself. "Besides, how could I? You don't think Stanislas Sadler would move his whole crew back to New York on the say-so of a simple sergeant. Even Captain Felix had a hard time convincing him."

Joe sighed with relief.

"In the end we provided the equipment and the crew. Sadler was so cheap he wouldn't even spring for film in the camera."

"No film?" Joe stared at her, then he started to laugh. "No film! Beautiful, really beautiful. That's my Norah, that's my girl, always one jump ahead."

"I'm not too happy about that part of it. Eilbott's confession, everything he did, the whole performance was for the camera. I knew there was no film in it. I cheated him."

"Ah . . . well, don't feel bad, love. It's the punishment he deserves. It may be the only punishment he'll understand."

183

"Probably."

There was an awkward pause.

"*Cara?* I shouldn't have walked out on you the way I did," Joe confessed.

"No, you shouldn't," Norah agreed.

That surprised him, but he went on. "I was wrong."

"I don't know what else you could have done that would have got through to me. I don't know how else you could have made me understand once and for all how much I'd hurt you." She sighed. "The whole thing went to my head—making sergeant, getting command of the squad. . . . I was too smart for my own good."

"There's nothing wrong with being self-confident."

"Except that I put everybody's back up."

"If you're talking about the job, you don't apologize for giving an order."

"I was going to get you reinstated, just me, single-handed. I ended up making things worse."

"No, you didn't."

"I wish I could believe that."

"You got Eilbott to confess to the crimes he committed and to disclaim guilt for the stabbing of Mrs. Waggoner."

Norah shrugged. "So?"

"So, I turned up a suspect for that one."

"You?"

"Why not? It was my case—once upon a time."

She flushed deeply. "I didn't mean it like that. I'm sorry. It's just that . . . well, you were supposed to be off the case. . . ." Then she saw that he was grinning. "What happened?"

"You remember that the very first reaction to the homicides at the Westvue was that they'd been committed during a robbery but that we couldn't prove it because we had no way of knowing what, if anything, had been taken. Okay. Now, do you remember the photos and posters Estelle Waggoner had of herself all over her apartment?"

"Of course."

"Did you happen to notice her wearing a big ornate brooch?"

"Sure. It was a great gorgeous piece of . . . junk?"

184

"That's what I thought at first," Joe agreed. "Fake, stage jewelry. She wore it in the poster she had of *The Merry Widow*, and it appeared in a couple of the other photos. Then, going through her theatrical scrapbooks, I spotted this same gold-and-ruby brooch again and again; didn't matter what the part was or the costume, the brooch was there. . . ." His smile broadened. "Right up front. So, on the chance, I checked through her insurance policies, and sure enough, it was listed."

"But you couldn't find it among her effects?" Eyes bright, Norah got to the point. "The killer stole it."

"Right. So I got a detailed description from the insurance company, had blowups made of the best of the pictures, and put the pawnshop detail on it. A couple of weeks ago they notified me that they'd located the brooch. That was one of the things I'd intended to discuss with you the night you were out on your date."

Norah opened her mouth to object.

"Of course, if I'd known who your date was. . . ."

"If I'd known you had a lead. . . ."

"I didn't even know you were back on the case. . . ."

They both stopped.

Joe took a breath. "Actually, I didn't have a suspect then, and I still don't. The guy who hocked the brooch gave a phony name."

"Naturally."

"But the pawnbroker remembers him and gave a pretty good description. As soon as Jim Felix realized that no way could your man and mine be one—"

"Why not?"

"Mine's black."

"Oh." Norah knew that Joe had had to pass the information on to Felix first, but what disturbed her was that the captain had not then told her.

Joe knew what she was thinking. "It was Chief Deland's decision not to tell you. Once we'd managed to separate at least one killing from all the others, Deland wanted to keep them separate. That way everybody saves face."

"It wouldn't have hurt to tell me," Norah said, then she

recalled the moment when Eilbott had offered to lie to clear Joe. Joe had already been cleared. She was glad she'd been able to turn Eilbott down without knowing it.

"With at least one other perpetrator involved in the West-vue killings, the chief can justify reinstating me."

Norah stared. "You've got your job back?"

"Yes, ma'am."

"Your same job? At the Fourth?"

"Yes, ma'am. I'll be back on Monday. And I thought . . . well, I know that the unit's been disbanded, so I thought you'd want to come back to Homicide. That is, you'd be working for me again. . . . Would you want to do that?"

"I'm not sure, Lieutenant." Norah took a deep breath. "I'd have to consult my husband. I could let you know . . . later tonight maybe?"